THE THIRD EYE

Living in Fear Series

They say it is a gift, I say it is a CURSE!

Be sober, be vigilant; because your adversary the devil, as a roaring lion, walketh about, seeking whom he may devour: Whom resist stedfast in the faith, knowing that the same afflictions are accomplished in your brethren that are in the world. 1 Peter 5:8-9 (KJV)

JRB ROSS

To order additional copies of this book, contact:
Xlibris
1-888-795-4274
www.Xlibris.com
Orders@Xlibris.com

Scripture quotations marked KJV are from the Holy Bible, King James Version (Authorized Version). First published in 1611. Quoted from the KJV Classic Reference Bible, Copyright © 1983 by The Zondervan Corporation.

Prayers and Rites of Exorcism are quoted within fair use from Catholic.org, "Rite of Exorcism"
https://www.catholic.org/prayers/prayer.php?p=683

ISBN: Softcover   978-1-7960-6598-5
         EBook   978-1-7960-6597-8

Print information available on the last page

Rev. date: 10/16/2019

THE THIRD EYE

Living in Fear Series

CHAPTER 1

HOW IT ALL BEGAN

I still remember as if it was yesterday, like a bitter taste that lingers in my tongue which I can't seem to get rid of. I was only 5 years old that time. Yes, 5 years old, but the trauma of the events that were about to unfold changed my life forever.

When I was young, my parents were both working to help each other out with the household expenses. There were still two of us siblings back then. My older sister Nancy, and me. My youngest sister was born when I was around 6 turning 7, I guess that's what I get foe being naughty *hahaha*!!!!

My parents would work from 8 in the morning till 5 in the afternoon leaving us with our Nanny which was kind of a norm in the Philippines. We had quite a number of nannies come and go that I lost track of all of them except for this particular one. Some people we encounter bring us either good or painful memories that stick with us all through our lives.

This nanny was weird, mysterious, mischievous, and silent. Never the less my parents trusted her, or maybe they just did not have a choice. She was in her mid-20s when she worked for us. Let us just call her "Sally". She came from a family that lived in a cemetery. This is quite common in the Philippines where homeless people would live in cemeteries. (Her parents were dead when she worked for us). Sally loves to wear black. Wore black lipstick, she had deep sad eyes, curly black hair, and teeth as yellow as gold. She was a woman of few words with a deep solid voice and scary smile.

My sister and I were very playful towards our previous nannies. I for one caused most of them to leave due to my naughtiness. I was a kid, and the youngest. What do you expect? I tried my pranks on her, but this was someone not to mess with.

One day, my parents already left for work and she asked us to go to the kitchen with her. Her hair was particularly messy that day; she had that mysterious and scary smile put on her face as she gently led us into the kitchen. I can tell she was on to something. Whatever that was, I didn't like it. She looked like she has not slept the previous night and she stinks as if she never took a bath for a week.

When we got to the kitchen, the light was off and all of the windows were shut close. There were candles lit in a circular position surrounding a bottle of Coca Cola in the middle. If I knew back then what I know now, I could have run and save myself a lifetime of misery. The air was heavy and it felt creepy. You could hear whispering voices running around the room. It was scary. It was as if the voices were speaking from inside your head. I started to get shivers down my spine. I was starting to get scared and my voice cracked when I asked her,

"What are we going to do here?"
"Oh Nothing, we're just going to play!
You and your sister better behave and do as I say or else you would have to face the consequences."
Damn, with those scary stare and frightening voice, we knew better than to argue! She asked us to kneel

with our heads touching the floor. We were in a circular position with the bottle of coke and the candles in the middle. I was so scared that my knees shake when I kneeled. I was breathing heavily and I swear I felt a little pee in my pants. She asked us to close our eyes and to never open them and just repeat whatever she says.

OoooWaaaaa!!!!!!!!!!!!!

YeeeOOOOwwwAAAAAaa!!!!!!!

She started singing and speaking in a language I do not understood. It felt like she blurting incantations as though summoning a great evil. I was so scared that my knees and shoulders were shaking pretty bad and my heart was beating like a drum. I wanted to cry. I am sure my sister was as scared as I was. I knew I heard a whimper escape from her mouth. With all the things she was doing, neither of us protested since we were too afraid of what she might do to us. I could feel a cold wind running around the kitchen, as if a wind was blowing from all directions. Her voice was starting to sound like the devil and I could not understand what language she was speaking. Could have been Latin, I don't know, I was so young that time I didn't any know anything about languages yet. Wait, it doesn't sound like her. No, it was not just her voice. The voice sounded demonic, sounded evil! There were more than one people talking and all of them are chanting in harmony. I felt the floor started to move but dismissed it as my legs were shaking uncontrollably. I tried to focus and tried to find courage within me.

Things started falling; now I was sure I could feel the room shaking. I could hear screaming coming from all direction that sounded like they were in terrible pain and in extreme agony! I was already crying but I could not dare open my eyes. I knew I was already peeing my pants, my knees and hands were all wet. I could not stand it any longer; I had to open my eyes! I needed to see light! I need to see my sister. I needed assurance that I wasn't alone. I opened my eyes expecting to see light but that was not what I saw. I thought it I was going to be relieved of the fear that I was feeling but when I looked at my nanny, what I saw was even a scarier sinister.

There was my nanny with her arms wide open and her hair blowing as if a wind was coming out of the bottle blowing straight in to her face. She was moaning this time with a look of pleasure and satisfaction in her face. Her feet didn't look like they were touching the ground. Was she levitating? I saw a black Silhouette in her back, which appears to be holding both her arms up. This was the silhouette of a devil. The two huge horns, which almost reached the ceiling. Bright red eyes that look like flames were escaping from them. My jaw dropped all the time and I just sat there frozen in fear. Then she sensed that I was looking at her. Her eyes suddenly opened wide. Slowly her head was moving to face me. When our eyes met, she screamed her heart out! Flies and insects coming out of her mouth. All the candles died and the bottle broke into pieces. I covered my face to protect myself from the explosion. Then there was a loud thug and I felt a pain in the back of my head. There were a lot of commotions going on and the next thing I know, she was on top of me! I caught a glimpse of my sister and she was crying. She was now sitting curled up in a corner but her eyes are still close. My nanny then grabbed a piece of the broken bottle. She looked up with her arms spread wide as if she was praying. She was murmuring something I don't understand and all the while I was pinned down on the floor. She then faced me with an insidious look. Pointed the sharp glass towards my forehead and slashed the middle portion. I felt a dull sensation between my eyebrows, and then it grew in to a feeling of burning like a fire flaming in my head! The pain was so intense that I finally collapsed.

CHAPTER II
SEX WITH THE DEVIL!

Since I was the youngest in the family during that time, I slept in the same bed with my mom and dad. We lived in an old ancestral house owned by my mother's family, built before the Second World War took place. The house was so spacious that it had to be divided in to four quadrants after their grandfather died, the upper left corner, upper right corner, lower left corner, and the lower right corner. We lived in one of the quadrants and each contain three bedrooms, one toilet and bath, a kitchen, and a living room. Customary to Filipino culture when kids are still young, my entire family all slept in the same room while Sally has the other room entirely for herself.

On this one cold and rainy night, I woke up to the sound of ferocious thunderclaps violently shaking the darkness of the night. The rain sounded savagely as it hits the roof like a thousand angry drummers determined to break the drumhead with their sticks. Just so you know, most of the houses in the Philippines are made of *"roofing irons"* so it's very noisy when it rains, making it impossible to hear anything unusual. All this noises and gave me an ill feeling which eventually gave me the urge to go to the bathroom, which is located near the kitchen. I was left with no choice and although I was scared to leave the comfort of our bed, the need to relief my self was greater than my fear.

I looked at both of my parents and they were sound asleep, they were peacefully sleeping despite all the commotions outside. I did not bother waking them up and disturb the calmness in their faces. To get to the bathroom, I had to pass by the Nanny's room which made it even creepier. The events that transpired the other day was still fresh in my mind. I finally gathered some courage to open the door, peeking before stepping out of the room, like a person who was about to cross a busy side walk. Normally, the hall way was dark, and nothing was ever visible.

This time it wasn't...

My Nanny's room was open and the light from her room was shedding light into the hallway. This should have made me feel better, I just don't know why it was giving me a tingling feeling instead. The thunder and the lightning never ceased and the noise of the rain continued. I tip toed as I walk, trying to avoid any sound as my tiny toes meet the wooden floor. I never should have gave in to my curiosity and avoided staring at her wide open door. Nothing could have prepared for what I saw. All the hair in the back of my neck stood, and my skin felt like it was separating from my bones, knees terribly shaking until I dropped to the floor because of the frightening sight in front of me. I sat their frozen, jaws dropped and unable to move. Fear fill my entire body and my heart violently beating....

I couldn't understand what was going on that time, my mind was still innocent and uncorrupted but what I saw was enough to give me nightmares. I saw Sally flat on her bed with her hands held up and her legs stretched wide open. She was smiling horrendously while staring blankly towards the empty ceiling, she was not blinking, her eyes were just rolling violently, her entire body continue to move in a forward-backward motion, as if something was pushing and pulling on top of her. With every push, she moans!

Why does she sound like she was feeling pleasure?

Another question running through my young and innocent mind was that, her room was totally lit by a fluorescent lamp but a dim shadow lay in front of her which takes a shape of some sort of an animal. It was a silhouette of a bull. Wait! No! It was not a bull! It was a humanoid with horns, no not human!!! It was a devil! When the beast came in to full figure, it was only then that I realized what it was. I saw the same devil days ago. It was on top of my nanny and it seemed as if he was devouring her. The devil's hand clamp against my nanny's arms, his filthy mouth sucking on her dark velvety neck, while its huge muscular body pinned my nanny down to the bed.

The innocence of my youth could no longer contain the frightening events unfolding before my eyes causing a scream to escape from my mouth. It inevitably caught the devil's attention.

Sudden pause..

Not a movement,

not a sound...

The noise from all the commotions outside caused by the rain seemed to have been placed on mute. All I could hear was the sound of bones cracking, breaking with every move of the devil's head which is slowly facing my direction. With an evil grin, I face now eye-to-eye with the devil as he continue to lay on top Sally.

"Those eyes!!!"

"Those horrible red burning eyes!!!"

From devouring my nanny, the attention shifted to me.

It slowly slid down the side of the bed, then slowly creeping, and crawling towards me. All the time my nanny remained smiling while staring blankly in the sky.

"Oh No!!!" What's it going to do to me?!! I'm gonna die!!!

The light was blinking on and off!

On Off   On   Off   On   Off

Everytime the light turns on, the devil's face came nearer and nearer. I called on Sally's name but she remained laying, still staring at the ceiling blankly, still smiling, motionless.

Lifeless?

Maybe....

The devil was about to reach me with its sharp dirty looking claws when our bedroom door suddenly swung open and out came my parents. They rushed to pick me up. They said I was screaming while sitting in the floor, bathed in my own piss.

Yes screaming,

like a girl!

What?

I looked around trying to find out what happened to the devil.

Where was it?

What happened to it?

Then I saw a pair of red eyes with sharp fangs smiling at me, slowly disappearing in the darkness of the kitchen. It was staring at me, as if saying.

"I'll be back!"

It took a couple of years before I realized what was going on at that time. Although she had her clothes on, my Nanny was having sex with the devil! The devil is an entity therefore; it need not take off your clothes when it penetrates you. My sister and I told our parents about all the things that have happened, and although good help was hard to find, they had to fire her. Thank God they did!

My parents realized that leaving their children with people of questionable background was not safe so my mother quit her job to take care of us.

Later on, I found out that she was pregnant with another daughter. Just recently, I heard from my mom that Sally died years ago. They found her lifeless on top of an empty tomb in the cemetery. The police could not make out what happened. There was no sign of foul play. She was just dead! Her eyes wide open and her mouth was mysteriously smiling. Hands and legs wide stretched but there was no sign of rape. If I knew then what I know now, she would still be alive, she would have been rescued from the shackles she was tied to.

CHAPTER III

PTEROCARPUS INDICUS

Locally Known in the Philippines as the "Narra Tree". Also known as "The bleeding tree"

NARRA - is the national tree of the Philippines. Known for the strength of its branch and mass of its trunks. Its trunk can reach up 2 meters in diameter and can grow as tall as 30-50 meters tall. Its fame does not just lay on its physical structure since it has also been subject to numerous horror stories on the internet due to the blood-like substance coming out of its bark when it is cut. Although, the blood like substance that comes out of its bark is nothing more than a tannin. Of course, I did not know it back then so I was greatly fascinated by it and always though the tree was alive, like a human.

I was on my first grade at this time, around 7 years old. Since I already had a sister and was no longer the baby in the family, I enjoyed a little independence and can now stay to play a little while at school before going home. I had a best friend named Carl who was my partner in crime.

To give you a little background, I was studying in a Public school founded by the Americans during their occupation in the Philippines. Even before it became a school, it was a mass grave for enemy soldiers. Due to the 2nd World War, the Americans just dug a huge mass grave where they throw the bodies if the dead Japanese soldiers. The lawn right next to the mass grave was where they properly burry allied soldiers which up to this day, is known as the "Veteran's Cemetery". Rumor says that the tree was haunted by the Japanese soldiers who were killed during the war, and their bodies remain buried right under that tree. Up to this day, the spirits of the dead still dwell in the tree, longing for proper burial, longing to get home, longing to take revenge...

In fact, a couple of years after I graduated from that school, the tree grew tremendously that grenades, rifles, helmets, and bones attached to the roots are exposing. The teaching staff noticed it and called the bomb squad who carefully dug the tree to secure the live grenades. The tree wasn't spared. After it was uprooted, mass possession terrorized the school. Hundreds of students would be possessed at the same time. It was such a huge story that it was even featured in national television. The event became uncontrollable so the possessed students were just taken to a nearby catholic chapel and hundreds of them were just laid on the floor until an exorcist came and performed exorcism on the entire school.

Before all of this, was our story..

Remember that popular proverb by Ben Jonson, *"Curiosity Killed the Cat"*. Well this story literally did, almost killed us.

One day, Carl and I got the best of our child plays when we agreed to do stay late after school until it becomes dark so we can do our investigation of the so-called haunted tree. Since it was a huge school, there were plenty of hiding places for use to choose from. We picked an old abandoned comfort room located next to a botanical garden. No one uses this room since it was scheduled to be demolished but the government might have forgotten about it, or they must have been busy with other stuffs. We weren't really afraid of getting caught specially that this school only hired one security personnel and only stays by the gate. The room was dark and hot, there was barely enough light for me to see Carl's reflection. We must have been really nervous or scared since we were just looking at each other's faces without saying anything. It was starting to get silent, as the noise of children playing from outside was beginning to subside. The only noise you could hear was the sound of our noses whizzing as we breathe. The silence was so deafening that it was starting to get creepy. I felt the urge to pee and was about to stand up when something grabbed me from my back. I fell down in the old wooden floor with a thug. I thug, I turned to my back to confront Carl why he would do such a thing.

"Why did you do that? What do you need? The noise could be heard by anyone from outside"

He remained silent, crumpled from where he was sitting, in the dark and cold corner on the floor without even looking at me. I felt a finger poking the back of my right shoulder I almost jumped when I realized it was Clark. His puzzled face met mine as asked, "who are you talking to? I was just here the whole time!"

The hair from the back of my head started raising and my neck became stiff. I slowly turned to see where the other kid was sitting to see who it was although I didn't. I was a bit relieved when I found out that he was no longer there. I didn't bother trying to seek for explanations and immediately started heading for the door. I could hear things crashing from our back so I started to run, I could see Clark was right behind me so I didn't stop at nothing until we reached the end of the door. It was only then that we stopped to catch our breath. We looked at each other without saying anything. I gave Carl a nod so he took out his bag and got our weapons ready. We were still kids but I could still feel the excitement mixed with anxiousness, and eagerness to experience the unknown. Armed with a rock, flashlights, waterguns, a bottle of Holy water that we got from our chapel, and we already felt like were the ghostbusters.

Darkness reigned and we decided to begin. The moon was bright that night, bright enough to light to our way. We slowly walked across the grassy school grounds that seemed to entangle with our feet every step that we take. I glanced by the gate and realize the security guard was no longer there. What is it? He must have gone for the day. I grabbed the flash light from my pocket and turned it on. No use, the darn thing might be broken. I tried to shake it with in my palm but it died anyway. Carl who was walking ahead of me, suddenly came to a stop and was looking up. I must have been so distracted that I didn't realize we were already there.

Right in front of us stood the Narra tree, thick leaves covering the sky like an umbrella, wrinkled branches like the back of an alligator, protruding roots rising from the ground like an insane octopus throwing his tentacles all over the place. Although we were scared to death, we also realized that we didn't come this far for nothing. We grabbed the holy water and filled it inside the water gun. First, we need to hit the trunk with the rock and once the bleeding begins, we were gonna spray it with the holy water using the water gun. Simple as that, a perfect plan. What we didn't realize was the consequence. We were so young. And dumb. And stupid. Who's gonna hit the tree and who's gonna spray the gun?

"Rock paper scissors!"

Unluckily, it was me who was gonna strike the tree with the rock. I took a deep breath, a sweat from my forehead fell in to the rock. I gathered my strength and my courage, raised the rock getting ready to strike. I'm not sure if I want to do this, so I closed my eyes and with a huge strike I hit the trunk as strong as my young arm could. I stopped after five strikes, fell back and took a great amount of oxygen for my lungs. Red fluid started flowing from its trunk like blood flowing from a fresh cut wound. It shimmered as the moonlight touched the liquid, sparkling, and dripping. It looked like real human blood, I was young but I had my fair share of childhood accidents so I was pretty familiar with blood from wounds. I felt an itch of guilt in my heart, why does it feel like I was hurting a human? Soon my guilt was replaced with an eerie feeling and was starting to feel uncomfortable.

A strong wind blew through the back of my neck. Something tells me terror is coming. We could hear dogs howling from a distance, as if they were afraid of something. These gave us goosebumps and cold wind started running down my spine. Fear filled my entire body causing my knees to shake a bit. I don't know if we should continue or just go home.

Too late..

Carl decided to sprinkle holy water into the wound of the tree.

Wrong Move….

Upon sprinkling, the wound from the tree started to smoke as if it was burning. Out of nowhere we heard an old man screamed, which shook us out of our wits! Was it the security guy? Was it a teacher? No this voice sounded like it was in Pain! Like it was in deep agony! The low moan is now turning in to a growl like it was filled with anger.

"Grarrrr!!!!!!!!!!!!!!!!!!!"

A sudden rush of strong wind, carrying dust, and dried leaves blew and knocked us into the ground. Our curiosity is now gone and is replaced by fear and remorse of our previous actions! We got up on our feet and started to run towards the gate but we couldn't! At first, I thought it was Carl pulling my leg, but when I looked back, it was a root! Or a branch maybe?

I don't know, up until today I still can't figure out what it was, everything's blurry when you're scared. What I can remember were a bunch of roots coming from the tree and it was pulling me. I called on Carl for help but I saw that it was dragging him too. It's pulling us towards the tree, dragging us across the grass and dust filled ground! The smoke coming out from the wounded tree was slowly taking shape forming a silhouette of a man. This time, strong wind was blowing from all direction, as if there was a hurricane. Then there were screaming! Voices coming from hell! Sound of great pain, anguish, and agony filled the atmosphere along with the commotions in the sky.

Everything became foggy, and the next thing we knew was that we were surrounded by a crowd of dirty looking people. No they didn't look like people. They looked like corpse! Hair soiled, clothes tattered, worms crawling from their faces in to their eyes and out of their ears, like the kind of scene you see in a zombie apocalypse movie. They were just there cheering, enjoying the view, looking at two agonizing naughty kids about to be devoured by an evil tree. A feeling of hopelessness befilled me, I never thought of dying young! I thought about my parents, my siblings, and my dog..

Goodbye world!!!

The ground where the tree stood broke open, exposing a glimpse of what hell looks like. Hands reaching out from inside the opening. They were just waiting for us to get there so they can grab us and drag us in to the ground with them.

With all the commotions and the rush of adrenaline caused by fear, I caught a glimpse of a boy who looked different from the rest of the crowd. He just stood there watching us. His face was so calm and clean, he seemed to be glowing. He pointed towards something on the ground near the tree. There it was, a bottle of holy water. When the bottle was about an inch away, I quickly grabbed it and sprinkled it towards the roots that is tied to my foot. It burned with the holy water causing for me to break free. I then stood up and did the same to my friend, Carl crawled his way in to safety. I went back to the tree and poured the remaining content of the bottle in to the opening. The earth was violently shaking as the ground slowly closed you. I remember horrible screams escalating from all over the place. They sounded like they needed help. The ground finally shut close and everything went back to normal. I looked at my friend's face, tears from his eyes colliding with the mucus dripping from his nose. He was crying, but this time, it was the cry of winning. It seemed like we had the same thing in mind. We ran for our lives towards the gate.

The next day I woke up with a very high fever. As expected, I was grounded. After that night of terror, we never spoke to each other again. I don't know why, but we just never spoke to each other ever again.

CHAPTER IV

THE VACATION

I was already 10 years old when this happened. It was summer break and my uncle invited me to spend my summer in their place. They live in a small island surrounded by white sandy beaches with crystal-clear blue water. I say small because the total land area is only about 21 thousand hectares. This was only a bonus. The reason why I want to spend my summer there is because of my two male cousins. They were around my age so we get along pretty good, and I love playing with them. I was the only boy amongst my siblings so I never really get to play with them.

What? You expect me to play Barbie's and doll houses.

After two hours of land trip, two hours by way of Bangka (small boat), I finally arrived! Oh yeah! Let the summer fun begin! My uncle's house was located right next to the school where his wife teaches. What separates the house from the school was a small barbed wire fence. My cousins showed me to their room so I could change and fix my stuff. I looked through the window and I noticed how they have a great view of the school from their room.

Something caught my attention. There was a jackfruit tree standing right beside a small fishpond. The tree seemed to bend giving a shed to the pond preventing the fish from dying of heat. There was something eerie about this tree, or was it just my phobia out of my past experience with the Narra tree. I don't know how to describe it, but lately, I've been a magnet to some bizarre happenings and supernatural events. My young mind tried to ignore these events, maybe I'm just imagining things.

I finished changing and went out of the room. My aunt and my uncle was about to head town because my aunt going to attend a teacher's conference in town, so, she advised us to stay in the house and not to leave while they are away. My cousins were so excited to take me to the beach that as soon as we heard the car engine start, they immediately jumped from their seats and began preparing for our escapade.

I lived in the city my whole life so all things provincial was something new to me. That could have been the reason why my cousins were so excited to show me around and take me to the white sand beach.

To get to the beach you have to go through a small forest, probably around a short fifteen to twenty minute walk. During that time, the island was less populated and the beautiful virgin beaches were still undiscovered. No investors yet which means everything is for free, no expensive hotel rooms, cottages, restaurants, pollutions, nor any tourists.

We arrived in the beach, and the short trek from the pocket forest absolutely paid off. The beach looked like paradise with its clean white sandy beach, coconut trees, and sparkling crystal clear blue waters! We hastily took off our clothes and throw them anywhere, we had the entire beach for ourselves. I took a dive in the cold water and saw school of beautiful colorful fishes swimming around that were not even afraid of our presence. Swimming naked was a pretty smart move to cover our tracks, so when we get home, no wet clothes to serve as evidence. We enjoyed playing in the water and had a good time that we totally lost track of time.

It was about to get dark when we realized that we had probably been there for hours. In panic, we put on our clothes, brushed the sand of our feet, and headed home as fast as we could. As we entered the forest, it was now pretty dark. What guided our way was the ray of moonlight escaping through the thick leaves of the forest trees. What should have been a 15 minute walk turned out to be an eternity! We have been running for more than 30 minutes now but still couldn't find our way out. My cousins knew the forest by heart but they've never been to it at night. With the concerned looks in their faces, I knew we were lost. We stopped for a while to make sure we were not going in circles. Suddenly, we heard footsteps, soft cracking of dead leaves and twigs behind us. We stopped for a while to listen, it was getting closer and closer. We looked around to see if it was an animal, but no! To our horror, emerging from a dark corner behind the bushes was an old woman staring at us with a sinister look. The way she stared at us looked like she had an evil plan in mind. She was slowly walking towards us with a walking stick on her left hand and something shiny on her right hand.

What was it?

As she came nearer, we realized she was holding a very large knife. It looked so sharp that it glittered when the moonlight touches its blade. We didn't wait to see what she was going to do and we ran as fast as we could. I tried to look back to make sure she wasn't following us. She wasn't. She just stood there, looking at us as we desperately tried to escape. Cackling. Laughing..

Nyehehehe!!!

Nyehehehe!!!

I read a number of Hansel and Gretel storybooks and had no idea I'd be in the same situation one day. It got me thinking nowadays; maybe that story came from real life experience. No matter how many books you read, nothing was going to prepare you for the real thing. What we saw was far more evil and scarier than the witch they portrayed. We ran until she was already out of sight. We only stopped to catch our breath. My heart was beating fast; it was beating like the sound of "George of the Jungle". My older cousin told us that we needed to take off our clothes and to turn it inside out. This is a belief in the Philippines; sometimes, "the others" play with you and mystify your sense of directions so you have to rearrange your clothes and wear it inside out to break the spell. After doing so, we started walking again. It wasn't long when we heard the cackle of the old woman. Oh no! She was following us again. How could she caught up with us? We were young kids with fast strong legs. How could her frail and gentle feet possibly gain that kind of speed? This time, we didn't hear her coming, what we heard instead were loud sounds of giant wings flapping. We looked up and I could swear it was the biggest bat I've ever seen in my whole entire life!

We started running again. My knees were shaking very badly and my feet were aching but we had to continue running. My heart was pounding pretty badly due to too much fear and exhaustion.

Hek hek hek hek!!!!

There goes that cackle again!!!

It was echoing throughout the forest. I looked up to see if "that thing" is still following us, but no. The coast was clear! It wasn't a bat! It was the old woman with wings like a bat! What made it more disgusting was that only half of her body was there. From the waist down there was nothing except for dangling intestines and bloody guts. I never believed in monsters as I thought they were just stories by my mother and my Nannies to scare us off to bed.

This one was real!

This was very real!

I prayed for this to be a nightmare, at least when I wake up, it will all be gone.

This one was real!

This was very real!

In addition, it was gaining on us!

We were running so fast. We were almost out of the forest, so in a desperate move,

the old woman made a dive to catch us but we ducked. Although, it was able to cut a portion of my shirt causing it to rip. I felt a sigh of relief,

"Good thing it wasn't my skin!"

We can see the road now; we were finally going to get out of this forest, this horrid jungle! We reached the road and flapping sound of the wings were gone. It didn't follow us out of the forest. What used to be a cackle was now an angry scream. I looked back and saw it crawling under a tree. Its hair was frizzy and messy, she almost look like she was Albert Einstein. Even with the darkness, I could still clearly see sharp fangs in her mouth. Her fingers were long and sharp, like Edward scissor hands. There was something in those long sharp fingernails; she looked like she was boastfully showing me a piece of cloth, which appeared to be the portion stripped from my shirt. She was intentionally showing me how lusciously smelled it, then she opened her mouth and a very long tongue came out of it, disgustingly licking the cloth. Her face, her looks, It was so unbearably evil that I eventually threw up.

We never stopped running until we were finally home. We got reprimanded pretty badly. We deserved it. I couldn't care much. I was just happy to be alive!

I Believed what we encountered was what we call "Mananaggal" which is one of the most popular monsters in the urban legends of the Philippines. Others may not believe it, I don't care. What we experienced was far greater than what an ordinary human brain can process.

After we ate dinner, we went straight to bed. We were pretty exhausted and dozed off right away. I woke up to the sound of my wristwatch beeping. Weird, I never set the alarm. I looked at my watch and it was exactly 12 midnight. I went to take a leak and went back to the room. As I prepared to get back to sleep, I accidentally took a peek through the window. I could see the jackfruit tree in the school; it looks as if the leaves are glowing. A Beam of light peeked through the leaves shedding light directly towards the fishpond. It was beautiful to look at. But wait! There is something else. There seems to be a white curtain shimmering, glowing, and beautifully sparkling as it danced above the pond. I rubbed my eyes to see if it was just my brain playing tricks on me. I could see it clearly now. It was a woman wearing a long white dress. Her silky white dress glitters with every touch of the moonlight. Long black hair flowing through her waist like a river flowing to the sea. I couldn't make out the face but with her skin glowing, and shimmering, captivated my eyes, you could almost picture her as a fairy.

Suddenly,

"Psst!"

"PssSsst!!"

It was one of my cousins.

"Get back to bed! She doesn't want to be seen."

"Why?" "Who is she?" "What is she doing out at this time of the night?"

"Just lay down I say!" my cousin's voice was more demanding now.

I glanced through the window again and I could swear the woman was looking my way. She was no longer dancing; she just stood there staring at me. Suddenly, she became furious as if somebody turned her beast mode on. Everything was blurry from afar, but I could swear she was getting ready to fly towards my direction.

In a matter of split seconds, her hideous face pressed through the window! Her jaw was wide open like it was about to drop! Blood dripping from her lips, ears, nose, and eyes! But what? There were no eyes! It was just pitch black! The hollowness of her empty eyes seemed so deep it felt like it was swallowing me in to a very deep pit. With the looks on her face, I could tell she was ferociously angry! She looked nothing like how I pictured her from afar. I dropped to the floor and crawled under the bed, I stayed there until morning.

The next day, my cousin told his mother about what happened last night and my aunt explained to me. *The story goes this way.*

There was once a young woman who got pregnant at a young age. Her boyfriend left the island after finding out about her pregnancy. To her shame, she hanged herself in that jackfruit tree. Since then, her spirit has been lurking and hunting the pond everything. Many attempted to get the tree blessed or destroy the pond, but anyone who attempted ended up getting sick. After several attempts, they decided to leave it alone.

That was a pitiful and creepy story. The rest of my vacation was ok. My advice, whenever you go on vacation on unfamiliar places. Always listen to the local's warnings.

CHAPTER V

THE HAUNTED HOUSE

Everyone left, my uncles, aunties, and cousins moved to new locations for different reasons. We were the only family left to live in the ancestral house so we decided to make the best of the space left. We moved to the upper left quadrant while boarders occupied the right side. In the Philippines, it is common for people living in the province to work in the city, rent a room, and just go home every weekends.

The lower left portion was converted in to a *carenderia.* A carenderia (in the Philippines) is a food stall with a small seating area where you can buy small portions of viands for a specific price. When my relatives moved out, creepy things started to occur. Will maybe it's been going on for a while but due to the house being crowded, we just failed to notice it.

-Gnomes-

My mother shared a story about her mother when she was still living; she used to have friends living in the attic. The attic was closed shut and no one has an access to it, no stairs, no openings, no nothing. It was believed to be inhabited by tiny little creature known as "gnomes" *(locally known as duwende).* My father dismiss her story, saying they were just "peeping toms". Maybe father never believed in those stuffs or maybe he was just trying to make us feel that there is nothing to be scared of, I don't know. At times, we could hear creatures running, giggling in the attic but my father would say there are just rats living there. I believed him, I mean, I tried to convince myself to believe him.

During my adolescence years, I used to sleep with one hand hanging from the bed. One night there was a power outage; this specific night changed my perception of things. This night, proved father was wrong. I woke to what sounded like children giggling from under the bed. That felt creepy since my sister was sleeping in my parents' room and there are no other kids in the house. I tried to focus, the sounds could be coming from outside. That wasn't the case, I am one hundred percent sure the sound came from under the bed. I could not understand what language they were speaking.

"Are they plotting to kill me?"

I felt the hair on my skin standing.

My eyes started to adjust towards the darkness; the light peeking through the window was not enough to give me a clear vision of what is going on. I don't know if it was my mind playing tricks on me, or it was just a dream. No it was not a dream, I blinked my eyes several times to be sure of what I was seeing, gnomes! I see gnomes! They were wearing some sort of a Santa hat, beard hanging from their chins, eyes glowing green, and the smell! They smelled like they haven't taken a bath in years. Suddenly, I felt my hand swinging and these little creatures were actually playing with it. They were giggling, singing, and dancing. I was too afraid to take my hand, for they might realize I was awake and they'd get mad. They did not sound aggressive; they even sounded playful and happy, but as human as we are, we have always feared what we don't understand.

I prayed for intervention, I was so scared and didn't know what to do so I just cried inside of me. Finally the power came back and the light turned back on. My eyes already adjusted to the darkness so when the light came back on, I couldn't see clearly right away, I did my best to open my eyes, just enough for me to see those tiny creatures running playfully, racing towards the bed. It took around five minutes for my eyes to adjust and for me to gather my thoughts, gathered some courage, before kneeling down the floor so I could peek under the bed. I leaned and saw nothing, they must have ran back to their hiding place. From then on, I never slept with my hand hanging from the bed. They still visit me from time to time but I kind of got used to their harmless presence.

-Agta-

-an agta is another creature in the Philippine folklore. It is an oversized evil creature ranging about ten to twelve feet, pictured as all black and is usually holding a huge tobacco-

On another incident, I was taking my evening shower. It was just a normal night, nothing out of the ordinary, so I wasn't expecting anything paranormal to happen. During this time, seeing ghost, spirits, and evil entities around is becoming normal. It only becomes scary when they actually make contact with me. I was so wrong to think this was going to be a peaceful night.

It was a warm day in summer and the feeling of cool water flowing from my hair down to my body was just so soothing. I was done with the shampoo, the soap, the toothbrush and everything but I left the water running since I was still enjoying the shower which felt so incredibly relaxing.

Then suddenly, a foul smell rose above the scent of the shampoo and the soap. It smelled like it was coming from a man that haven't taken a bath in ages! So disgusting, I almost threw up. On top of this was a very strong scent of tobacco, which I tried to rationalize due to my father who sometimes smokes in the house. I looked around to see where the smell was coming from, and that's when I noticed a pair of red glowing eyes lurking by the window staring at me. It was just a small rectangular opening with no cover of any sort, no curtains, and no blinds. This window was facing our empty backyard, surrounded by trees and a tall fence; all you could see outside was pitch black and nothing else. Therefore, I was puzzled as to how this hideous creature got there. There was a scary ugly face to go along with that pair of red glowing eyes. The face looked like it was covered in charcoal, with an overgrown beard and mustache, which looked like santa claus, except it was black, frizzy, and dirty. It had a sinister look and had a very frightening evil smile with yellow teeth. It let out a soft laugh when he realized I was looking at him. His evil laugh was something that would hunt me for years. His voice was heavy and loud, it sounded like the voice of serial killers you see on movies. I initially stood there, frozen in fright, trying to understand what I was looking at. Then it hit me, I felt a vibration ran from my feet in to my hair and I screamed. I bolted outside of the bathroom naked; the only thing covering my private part was a dipper. I sat there in the corner shivering and shaking. I was too scared and could not utter a word. My parents were shaking me with concerned looks on their faces but I could not say anything. Traumatized! That's how you can describe me at that time. It couldn't be any man playing pranks on me, the comfort room is located in the 2nd floor and there is no way a normal human can climb that wall. Besides, it was a gated empty lot, no one goes in and out except us, and what about those glowing red eyes?

-White Lady-

On a separate incident, I slept without taking a shower due to the "agta" incident. It was very uncomfortable since it was summer in the Philippines and the temperature can go as high as 107.96°F. Thanks to my daily tasks and to-do-lists, I still managed to doze off that night. It was a night to remember.

I was peacefully asleep when suddenly I woke up to the sound of my bedroom door creaking. Nowadays, I was so sensitive with their presence that it's becoming impossible to ignore them.

EeEEEeeeeeeekkk...

It was slowly opening, as if whoever was sneaking down there is trying to make sure I stay asleep so he can kill me. This confused me, the method is that if a serial killer but the presence tells me its paranormal. Maybe I was just overthinking, maybe it was just my mom checking on me. I Don't know, the suspense is killing me!

The door suddenly swung open and hit the wall with a bang! There was no one there so I pulled my covers, thinking it may be those tiny creeps again, I pretended to sleep. I stayed vigilant and sensitive from all the noises and sounds around me. I tried to control my breathing, tried to control the beating of my heart, waiting for a sound or a movement. There was none! My sheets were suddenly pulled making me feel like the most naked man on the planet. I continue pretending to be asleep but I gotta tell you how herculean it was to pretend to be asleep in that petrifying event. The horror did not stop there, it must really be desperate to get my attention that it was trying to wake me up.

Suddenly there was another Bang! It wasn't coming from the door. Was it the door again? I slightly opened my eyes, just enough for me to peek and see what was going on. It was the window. An unseen force is slowly opening the window then closing it with a bang! This is a wooden jalousie type window, which means it is very tight and cannot be opened or closed easily. It also has a mosquito net, so no one from the outside can open or close it from the other side except inside the room.

This was a very old house and each movement causes wood to produce a creaking sound, so each time the window is move, the creaking sound contributes to the creepiness and fright I feel.

It went on and on,,,,,,

CreeEEkkkkkkk!!!!!!!!!!!!!

BAnngg!!!!!!!!!!!!!

CreEeeEkk!!!

Bang!!!!!!!!!!!!!

It was getting more violent now! I waited for help. No, not waited, I longed for help! Where are my parents? Can't they hear this? And what's that smell? Oh!!! There goes that smell again! So foul! So disgusting!

Then I heard an evil grin, an evil laugh! It could have smelled my fear and realize I was awake that's why it was laughing at me. I wanted to cry, It was driving me crazy, I wanted to pull all my hair out! I wanted to run! Instead, I just froze there in terror. Too afraid to move! If this was a dream, I hoped I wake up. I pinched myself several times, robbed my eyes and nothing happened. No this wasn't a dream! This is for real; this is haunting me, a real life horror movie.

I don't know if this night was ever going to end, so out of desperation, I snapped... When a person reaches his boiling point, his fear disappears and is replaced with rage. So how exactly do you show rage against an evil entity? You use the very thing that drives them away, and it is your faith in God. I stood up, it was only then that I finally saw what was haunting me. It was a lady dressed in all white, with long silky black hair, waving as if a wind is blowing towards its face. Deep gray lonely eyes and lips as pale as snow. I made the sign of the Cross and on the top of my lungs I prayed the Lord's Prayer. I prayed with the loudest voice I could ever produce.

Our Father which art in heaven, Hallowed be thy name.

Thy kingdom come, Thy will be done in earth, as it is in heaven.

Give us this day our daily bread.

And forgive us our debts, as we forgive our debtors.

And lead us not into temptation, but deliver us from evil!!!! -KJV

After completing the prayer, the banging suddenly stopped. Just like that. My parents were suddenly by the door asking me what just happened; they were questioning me why I was shouting in the middle of the night. I told them everything but they told me all they could hear was my shouting and no other noise.

From then on, I realized how powerful this prayer was. This is the Lord's Prayer taught by Jesus Christ Himself. Therefore, if ever you're caught in a situation like this, you know how to handle it. Although, I could have handled it better now that I think about it. That was a lost spirit that was desperately in need for my help, but what was I to do? I was to young back then..

CHAPTER VI
MOVING OUT

With all the things going around, It seemed like this house is cursed after all. On top of all the paranormal things going on, we were also experiencing series of bad lucks which I attributed to the negative entities living in our house. Water and electricity cut off, job loss, and business bankrupcy. Even our neighbors have their fair share of paranormal experiences in this house. You don't need to have your third eye open, just by simply entering the house it will give you the creeps right away. Although, if yours are opened, you'd be crazy I'm sure.

Melvin,

One night I was drinking with your father. I was so drunk that I could not walk home anymore so I passed out in the billiard table. I woke up in the middle of the night, looked at my watch, it was about 12 in the morning. The lights were off. I waited for a moment for my eyes to adjust to the darkness and I could see your father passed out in the chair beside the pool table. Suddenly there was a soft cackle coming from under the table. It sounded like it was coming from a witch. I tried to look down to see if it was one of our drinking friends playing tricks on me. What I saw that night was the most horrifying sight I have ever seen in my entire life. Nothing could have prepared me for the horror I was about to witness. There it was, an old woman with red glowing eyes. Blood dripping from her lips as it sucked on a life-less rat. It raised its head and looked towards my direction. Our eyes met! Then it let out an angry scream! I saw her jaw stretched like it was about to hit the floor, man! It could swallow my head if it wanted to. I jumped and fell down the table. I ran as fast as I could barefoot in to the street as far away from your house as possible. Since then, I never came back to your house, even to collect my slippers.

Brandon,

I was in your back yard, with your father's permission of course. I needed to try out my new "UTG mil-dot" scope for my pellet gun. I was trying it in your back yard since this place was enclosed and gated so there was no danger of anyone entering in and out of the property without passing through the front door. I placed the can in the other end of the bricked wall. I positioned as far away as possible before sitting in a comfortable position, and then peeked through the scope. The distance was perfect. I took my eyes of the scope and took a deep breath. The site was crystal-clear as if the target is within my reach. Out of nowhere a white figure passed by the target, so I took my eyes off the scope, put down the gun to make sure there was no one near the target. To my surprise, no one was there. I was alone; all you could hear was the sound of the birds chirping. A cold wind started running down my spine. I tried to ignore it and put my eyes on the scope again. The thin can came in to view when suddenly; a face peeked through the other side of the scope. I was so surprised that I fell down on the ground. The face looked pale as an ice, long hair covering its face exposing only one eye. The eye looked angry like it was in rage. It remind me of the movie "The Grudge". I looked at its direction but it was nowhere in sight. When I looked to my left, there it was with her angry hideous face just inches away from my ear. She screamed in the loudest most horrific way. I picked up all my stuff and ran out as fast as I could. I don't remember saying goodbye to your parents and I don't remember going back to that dreaded place ever again.

Cop,

I was renting the flat opposite to the apartment you and your family were staying in. Being single that time, I would bring different girls almost every night. I had 3 terrifying encounters in that house, in which the 3rd one finally made me leave.

First encounter= I was sleeping at that time when I was awaken to the sound of tiny laughter. Since I sleep with the lights on (occupational hazard), I could clearly see tiny human creatures with Santa hats and long beards sitting by the table. They were watching me while I was sleeping. I reached out for my gun and they all scrambled running under the bed. I followed them with my terrified eyes and when I looked down, they were nowhere in sight.

Second encounter= I picked up a girl from a local bar. We had a few drinks and decided to crash in my place. We entered my room and started kissing. From what I could tell, this girl was around the ages 20-25 years old. She had a short, straight, black hair. Cute nose and pouty lips. I bit those lips, slowly my hands reached down to grab her round ass while my chest collided with her perky breast. I kissed her all the way down to her neck while my hands continue its voyage around her panties. She wore a sleeve-less shirt making it easier for my tongue to run from her ear into hear neck, down to hear cleavage. I removed her shirt and bra. I was sucking her nipples and was sucking it dry, I was like a hungry infant with an appetite of a full grown man except there was no milk. I kissed her lips again and my tongue started tangling with her tongue. Meanwhile my fingers found its way into her paradise, 1 finger, 2 fingers, 3 fingers until it was very wet and she was moaning like she was about to come. I tore her panty off and tossed her to bed. Like a hungry dog I removed my shirt and pants and started diving in to her. I could feel our breast collide as I plunged deeper in to her. I was drowning in pleasure when suddenly she let out an evil giggle.

What was that sound? That did not sound like her.

I got distracted and when I looked at her face, it was not her face anymore. Her face transformed from a brown cute faces lady in to a corpse. Yes, a rotting corpse, like she's been dug from the grave, she was smiling, her dead eyeballs were looking at opposite directions like a cross-eyed bitch. She had crooked yellow teeth stained with tar or mud maybe? I don't know. With that scary and nasty look on her face with blood all over her face, damn it was impossible to think straight! I jumped out of the bed like a naked frog which surprised her. She gave me a blank stare. Her face became normal again. I put on my clothes; I lost the appetite for sex. She was complaining and was grumbling as she was putting her clothes back on. The bitch wanted more! I can't really blame her, we were just getting started. She told me it was the worst date ever and left, slamming the door behind her. I reached out for a bottle of beer from the fridge and looked out the window. I saw her hail a taxi. I was still confused about what just happened. I just stood there trying to make out of what happened. I drank the entire bottle like it was water. I reached for another bottle of beer. The cold liquid slip through my throat giving me a feeling of comfort. When I finally had my fill, I decided to go back to my room to sleep. I opened the door of my room and was welcomed by a foul smell that seemed to have come from a decaying flesh. I'm a cop, so I definitely know what a rotting a dead body smells like. Upon turning the light on, I was exposed to a terrifying view of a rotting corpse there on the bed. The zombie looking lady spoke with her cracking voice,

"Are you ready for another round?"

I passed out....

Third Encounter= I thought that was the worse, and I wished it was. I should have moved out after that experience. Now the third encounter got me running out of the house and only came back the next day to collect my things. It was like that movie "Amityville Horror" where they were driven out of the house in the middle of the night.

This is the story...

I came home early one night since I had to attend an early morning assembly the next day. I decided to sleep early and set my alarm clock to 4:00 am. I was very tired that day so sleeping early doesn't seem to be a problem. In the middle of the night, I woke up to an excruciating pain in my butt. It was like an intense pressure was pressing in and out of my anus. I tried to move but I could not.

I was lying flat on the bed with all hands and legs pinned down. The pain was so intense, the bed was also shaking it felt like someone was fucking me from my behind. Something was definitely fucking my behind. Then I heard a demonic laughter echoing through the room.

Grahahahahaha....

Bwahahahaha!!!!!

Suddenly, everything stopped except for the throbbing pain in my butt. Everything was still, no movements, no more laughter. I still could not believe what just happened. I could feel my Butt swelling from the pain. I just got butt-fucked by a demon! I had to leave the house in the middle of the night and stayed with a friend. I was ashamed to tell him of what happened. What was I to say?

-special note, the room that this cop is renting, was the same room where I saw my nanny having sex with the devil.

Mom,

I never really wanted to move out of the house. This belonged to my great grandparents. There are too many precious memories here. Although some included creepy ones. I remember when I was in college; I constantly stayed up late at night to study. I would study in the kitchen table opposite to the window. The windows back then were sliding windows made out of wood and shells. I was very serious and focused that I did not notice it was already passed 12. Determined to get high scores on my exams, lost in the pages of my books when I noticed something white, like a lady in her night gown passed by the window. It would have been impossible for someone to walk there since it was in the 2nd floor, so most likely she would have to float. I tried to ignore it and went back to my studying again. This time, in my peripheral view I noticed it again, it was trying to get my attention so this his time I turned my head out of curiosity. It was then that I saw a woman wearing all white floating by the window. The woman had a very pale skin with no eyes. It was just hollow. Her eyes were waving like a wind was blowing straight towards her face. She was inviting me to come join her, she raised her hand inviting me come hold it. I moved the chair a little to get me an extra space, just enough for me to be able to get up. All the time I never removed my eyes from her as I slowly got up from the chair. I assessed the situation, the path was clear! I sprinted out of the kitchen and ran to my room. I never studied in the kitchen again!

Going back, I knew that if we leave the house, it would be easier for our surviving uncle to sell the property. Everybody have to sign but if we step out, majority would be in favor of selling it. Here is what really pushed me to step out....

I woke up one night. The house was shaking like there was an earthquake. The entire house was extra foggy and bright, like I was walking in a dream world, as I stood up, I could see my physical body asleep right next to my husband. I cautioned him to wake up but he only winked for a second without acknowledging my presence and went back to sleep.

Maybe he couldn't see me?

Has my spirit separated from my body?

I went pass the wall to my son's room, he was awake and he was staring at me as if he was seeing a ghost. I just smiled at his surprised face and continued. Somehow, I know that the quake was coming from downstairs. I went passed the door like from the movie "hollow-man"! There was a blinding brightness coming from the lower part of the house seems to intensify as I get nearer and nearer. I went to the source of this blinding whiteness, and there it was, an image of Our Lady of Fatima slowly turning to face towards my direction. A soft, comforting, angelic voice came out of her moth as she spoke the following words:

"Get out of this place, this is no longer home to you. This place houses many dark entities that's hindering blessings from coming in"

The next day I told my family about the apparition. To my surprise, my son validated my story and told me he saw me passing by his room through the walls. I took this as a sign and I knew it was time to leave the house...

CHAPTER VII
GHOST IN THE UNIVERSITY

When I attended high school in this university, the building was very old and most of the materials were made out of wood. Due to the creepy structures and buildings, it was inevitable for stories of paranormal to circulate around the campus. There have been rumors of ghostly sightings in this school but you never really pay much attention to it when you're young and eager and excited.

One of the rumors was about a beautiful student who committed suicide by jumping from the sixth floor of the high school building. Then an unfortunate thing happened, our school building burned down. Rumor has it that there was a man burned to death. It was a professor who have been with the school for four decades. They say this professor was rumored to be a womanizer, targeting his students as his prey. They say, he even impregnated a student once and that woman jumped off from the building. Did the woman finally get her revenge? Anyway, it was heart breaking especially for the owner of the school. Heavy heart filled with sadness and tear flowing from his eyes as he helplessly watch the building slowly burn to ashes.

"We will rebuild" were the words that came out of his mouth, full of conviction and determination. An entire school year has gone so fast, I was now on my 2nd year in high school and the new building was now ready for occupancy, just in time for the opening of a new school year. It was a 6 story building, which was already tall during that time. The 6th floor was an open area which was where P.E. classes were held. It got a great view of the city, with red and yellow lights flickering from distant vehicles that looked like stars twinkling in the sky. In Philippines, it is customary to have a building blessed by a priest or a pastor to drive away evil spirits before occupancy. Although the building was ready, it was not yet occupied since it wasn't blessed yet.

One day, I and my buddy agreed that we would sneak in the new building to be the first to experience the view from the 6th floor. We planned to wait until most of the students are already gone for the night so that the security personnel would then be tucked in their barracks enjoying their coffee and donuts. I guess I never learned my lesson from my experiences from my previous school. Everything worked just as we planned. It was a good thing that there were no CCTV's yet during that time so nothing could get in the way of our amazing plan. Sweating, panting, and dragging every step, things we had to endure just to fulfil our curiosity. Not to mention the ducking occasional and listening to sounds to make sure the guards don't catch us, like James Bond on a secret mission. When we finally reached the 6th floor, it was all worth it. The wind was cold and the view was fantastic. The rush of adrenaline flowing through our veins have been calmed by the breath taking view. Carbon dioxide in our lungs were slowly being kicked out and replaced with the cool wind rushing through our nose providing such a relaxing and soothing sensation.

It was good to watch the city lights from a distance, people walking along the side walk, and distant noise from cars honking. I don't know about my friend but I was enjoying the moment. Never did it occurred to me that the stillness of the moment would be broken by an un-identified horror. Out of nowhere, I heard a sound of a lady sobbing. It seemed like she was crying right next to me. Her scary voice flows through the opening of my ears and her breath touched the hair on the back of my neck, spiraling down my auricle. I turned to my friend to see if was experiencing the same things and he gave me that "I feel it too" look. A cold chill ran down my spine, like an ice cold water poured in my back. I felt my heart beat accelerating, like a beat slowly changing from mellow in to a rock song. Trying to reason with myself, trying to not be hasty with my conclusions, it could have been just another student, or it could have been senior students who decided to play pranks towards these wonderers. Never the less, we turned to check where the cry was coming from, trying to make sense of this horrid happening. As we turned to investigate, there it was, a female student sitting in a dark corner sobbing while covering her face with her palms. A slight comfort filled our heart knowing that it was just another student.

We felt relieved and we both agreed to approach her and see what her problem was. Boys will be boys, so we were even teasing each other as to who will be able to take home the broad.

"I'm gonna take one for the team man."

"No man, I saw her first"

"But it is my idea that we approach her"

"nah, may the best man wins"

"hahaha".

Slow excited steps as we got closer to the lady. We asked her what was wrong as I placed my hand towards her back as a gesture or an assurance that she was not alone and we are her to comfort her. When my hand touched her soft back, I realized she was extremely ice cold! Not minding the two idiots ganging on her, she ignored us and continued to sob. Taken aback by the foul air running through my nose, I noticed that the lady smelled awfully bad, she smelled like a dead rat! I gave my friend that "she's all yours" look. This time, he bent down and moved his face closer to hers as he asked him what was wrong. Her hair was covering her face so we couldn't really make out what she looked like. Her appearance remains a mystery which added to the creepiness piling up in my questioning mind. Maybe my friend could not feel it, but I've had pretty close encounters with spirits and entities, and this one. Well, I wasn't sure yet, but my guts tell me she's one of them.

I noticed her head was staring to move. It was scary how she slowly lifted her head to face us. Every split second, every movement was torture. It felt like hours before we could get a full view of her pale face, plus, plus, the dimness of the light was really not helping. It was really scary but I don't know why we stayed. Our eyes were simply locked to her dead ugly face. Maybe it was curiosity, maybe our bodies were just paralyzed with fear, I don't know, maybe it was just fate. I almost jumped out from where I was standing when her bone-chilling face came into full view. Her eyes were empty, like it was a void swallowing our souls in to a deep abyss. I stared at it for a good few seconds and I couldn't look away like a shackle is stranded to my neck in to her face. Blood slowly flowing from her head to her face shedding color to the once pale face. Her sobs now echoing throughout the place, piercing deeper in to my ears, lunging down to my soul. It was all I could hear, it was like being devoured in to an ocean of loneliness, like the crying was coming from inside my head! Even with all the horror we were in, my brain tried to manage what was in front of me and I noticed that her face was broken like she got hit by a car or fell off a building. Fell off a building, that's right! I remembered the rumor about the lady who jumped from the building, splattering her brain all over the ground floor. Somehow I came to my senses and managed to stare away from her eyes. My friend was still frozen in fear, staring at her face with jaws dropped and eyes wide open. I managed to pull my friend and he was slowly regaining his senses. We managed to find the wit to finally get the hell out of that place. We were now running down the stairs. Skipping steps. Flying between levels. I could still hear her crying inside my head, and the fear clouding my mind is slowly going away.

Everything is now making sense. That lonely spirit we encountered was calling her mom, desperately seeking help. The heavy feeling in my heart is not fear, it was a sense of pity, she was able to channel her emotions to me and I felt her pain. She longs to reunite with her mom so she can ask for forgiveness. This distressing figure might not be here to scare us but to ask for our help. Never the less, there was nothing I could do. I'm sorry, I'm just a kid and my fear is greater than my desire to help.

It took almost an eternity before we finally reached the first floor. We stopped by the ground floor to catch our breath, trying to regain our composure.

"What are you kids doing here?" A loud voice echoed through the hall way. Instead of being afraid that we may get in trouble, I was somehow relieved to hear a grown man's voice. Never have I been so glad to be found, like we were being saved from drowning.

I turned to where the voice was coming from. Just when I thought all the horror and consternations was over, I was wrong, so wrong, for a zombie looking figure was dreadfully limping his way towards us. He looked like he was burned with his skin hanging from his face exposing his skull and tattered clothes dangling from his body exposing his grilled body. This man was burned pretty good. It may take some time before I ever eat any grilled meat again! But how could he still be walking? We just lost it. We gave up on making sense of everything that was going on and decided to race with each other, out of the school, the gate as our finish line.

Needless to say, we never stayed late in school again. . .

Years passed and I managed to stay away from any opportunity of meeting those two blood-curdling creatures again. I finally reached senior year where I became the class president and was a vice-president of the entire high school department's student body organization. I used to come to school early to do extra-curricular activities, thinking early is better than staying late.

When I entered our classroom it was no longer empty which was unusual. I noticed that one of my female classmates was already there leaning in her desk. This raised a question in my mind since it was still 10 in the morning and our class was scheduled to begin by 12:30 noon time. She looked like she was lost in her slumber. Her long black hair flowing through her desk providing cover for her face. The only movement present was the occasional raising of her back due to her breathing. Curiosity filled me since I couldn't make out who it was. Making my way in to the spaces between the tables so I planned to disturb her nap and do a little chit-chat. She might just be bored that's why she decided to do a little nap time. I decided to gently tap her arms, but when my hand touched her skin, I was taken aback. She was ice-cold! Like she just got out of the freezer after being stuck for a long time. It was a familiar feeling.... Her head slowly turned 180 degrees creepily facing me like her neck was an elastic rubber but with the sound of bones cracking and breaking. She gave me the most insidious smile that still appear in my nightmares, it was the same lady from the 6th floor....

Her smile disappeared and her face suddenly transformed in to a dreaded looking corpse before finally screaming

MAMA!!!!!!!!!!!!!!!!!!!!!!

CHAPTER VIII
GHOST IN THE UNIVERSITY

Part II

The Comfort Room: I went to college in one of the oldest universities here in our town. This university is known for the quality of education and state of the art facilities although some of the buildings are old, they managed to equip the school with modern facilities suitable for the modern world. Foreign missionaries established the university after the First World War making it subject to rumors about ghost of priests and nuns lurking around the premise. I never put any of this in mind.

I was now in college, I was very anxious being in a new school, new environment, and new people. My first class begins as early as 7 in the morning and it was still early so I was lazily climbing the stairs to our classroom which was located on the top floor of the building.

Since I live near the university, I was already there as early as 6. I loved feeling the cold morning breeze running through my nostrils, the chirping sound of the birds trying to feed their young, and the beam of sunlight escaping through the clouds making its way to my skin. I was the only one there, being a Filipino, this already considered early. Sadly, this is one of the bad habits of Filipinos, most of us are always late. We call this "Filipino time" where we agree to meet at seven, but eventually arrive at eight.

I finally reached the eight floor and did a little thinking, I never really liked this course I'm studying but this is what my aunties wanted. If I had my way, I would have taken that scholarship and studied business management. Due to the orange juice I had for breakfast, my anxiousness, and the cold wind running through my lungs, I felt the urge to pee.

Luckily, the comfort room was just located right next to the classroom. I opened the door and the smell of old rotting wood with spider webs dangling from the ceiling welcomed me. It was creepy but I still went in and took a piss. I know I was alone when I entered the premise but why do I feel like I wasn't, like someone was watching my every move, like a strange spine-chilling presence was there with me.

Suddenly a hushing sound came out from the closed cubicle along with a cold wind which ran down my spine giving me that strange harrowing feeling. Small bumps started raising in my arms and the hair in my skin started to erect when I heard someone whisper in my ear. What was it? Who was that? I could not make out what it was saying so I did my best to ignore it. I have my college course to think about and I thought all these bizarre events were behind me when we moved to a new house and I transferred to a different university. I tried to avoid any sudden moves, nor did I make any disturbing sound so as not to disturb the surreptitious presence lurking there. When suddenly the tranquility was broken when all of the toilets were flushing together by its own. I got out as fast as I could even if I wasn't done taking a leak, my penis exposed showering urine all over the floor. I made it out, zipped my pants, and shut the door behind me. Luckily no one was there yet, so I did my best to stay as far away from the comfort room as possible while waiting for everyone else to arrive. Students started arriving followed by our instructor. She was a nun who looked to be in mid-50s. Class started and she divided us in to groups. We were instructed to introduce ourselves to one another like what they normally let us do during first day of classes.

Most of the girls from the group I was in knew each other since they graduated high school from this university. One of them with the most outgoing personality shared a story that shook me from my seat. With a serious expression on her face, one could tell that what she was about to say was true, as she looked each of us in the eyes. Her voice cracked as she spoke in a whisper like manner as to prevent someone or something from hearing what she was about to say. She revealed to us that the comfort room in this floor, the one located just outside the classroom was so haunted that they had to close it permanently and seal the doors. I informed her that it was impossible since I just used it earlier before everyone arrived, but I never mentioned to her what happened to me. Her expressions changed as she laughed and though that I was actually kidding. Her conviction about her story was great, she was affirmative the doors were sealed and students were advised not to use it. She was even present when they closed and sealed the doors. I know better than to argue but this recent discovery leaves a gyre of confusion in me. I couldn't wait for the class to end so I can investigate for myself and fill the void left in my brain from un-answered questions.

Did I imagine everything that happened earlier? Did they finally fix that dreaded comfort room and had it re-opened?

After the class, I waited for everyone to leave so I can go there and check again. After making sure that the coast was clear, I slowly made my way in to the comfort room in question. To my horror, she was right! The door was shut and nailed against the wall. By the looks of it, one can really see that it was nailed a long time ago. The nails hid under the old faded paint with cobwebs dangling against the door frames and the door. My curiosity and yearn for a logical answer did not stop there as I grabbed the knob and tried to open the door. She was right again! It's locked. This venture for answer fired back and left me with even more questions that remained unanswered up to these days.

The Nun: My visions and sightings of paranormal phenomena drove me to be closer to God even more. I discovered that any malignant presence and entities cannot touch me as my faith grew stronger. One of my conquest led me to be a member of a religious youth groups. Being a catholic institution, the university strongly supported our organizations that they even provided us with a dedicated meeting room. We would meet once a week after our classes to pray, sing songs of praises, and share the word of God. Well, the negative entities still try to disturb me or get my attention on several events.

On this particular event, it was around 5 in the afternoon and the sun was about to set, darkness slowly creeping its way around the campus. On our way to the meeting room, we were talking about something really funny and everyone was hysterically laughing as we walk. I had the key to the meeting room and when I opened it I saw a nun facing the altar. The room was pitch black except for the dim lights coming from the electronic candles in the altar which sheds just enough light for me to see the frightening figure. She didn't look like she was praying, she sounded like she was murmuring with frustrations visible even with her faint face. I closed the door again and advised everyone to be quiet as there was a nun praying inside. Our leader made his way to the front and advised me that no one else uses the meeting room except us. Gathering all my wits and courage as I slowly twisted the knob before finally swinging the door wide open. The entire room came in to view and gladly there was no one there.

There's only 1 door leading to and from this room so she would have to pass through us if she had gone out. It must have been a product of my imagination so I decided to let it go and everyone went inside.

We began with a solemn prayer, sang songs of praises, and then started our sharing session. One of our members was emotionally sharing when I suddenly caught a glimpse of what looked like an old woman standing in the corner right next to me. I tried to feed my curiosity by looking toward its direction only to see that it was the same nun I saw earlier. She was standing in the corner with her head down. She was wearing a white long sleeved shirt, navy blue skirt, and a white veil. When she realize I was staring at her, she became extremely ferocious and gave me the loudest growl I have ever heard in my whole entire life. Some of this entities really hate to be seen and some would intentionally draw your attention. I got a good look at her insidious face and could see that she had very dark eyelids with eyeballs occupying the entirety of her eyes so that no white can be seen. Her face was so grey and pale with veins cracking from every corners of her face. Black cracked lips as if she used charcoals as lipstick. Her aggravation elevated and it's evident how motivated she was to take it to the next level since she is now coming forward to attack me. Her dirty skinny hands were ready to strangle me, it looked powerful enough to break my neck. As a defense mechanism, I was taken aback causing me to fall from the chair. I quickly picked myself up and immediately ran outside. Although none of them could see her, everyone decided to run along with me.

I think it was around 7 in the evening so the campus was now empty. Except for the lights in the hall way, the rest of the surrounding was pitch black. I stopped in front of the abandoned elevator to catch my breath when the damn thing suddenly swung open. Thick white fog came out followed by the nun's horrendous face still raging with anger. The others finally caught up and we ran all the way down the stairs until the gate came in to view. Gasping for air, trying to exhaust the remaining energy and oxygen left in our lungs, we never stopped until we were finally outside of the school and away from the appalling creature.

We were breathing heavily, hearts beating like drum, knees still shaking from the non-stop running and we could only look at each other in the eyes.

Upon recovering from the deep exhaustion, I finally got the nerve to explain to them what happened. I need not give a deeper explanation since they also shared to me what they felt the moment we entered the meeting room. The room's temperature was hot but a cold wind would blow from the back of their heads from time to time although the door was close and there was no fan or air-condition system. Before I ran, they also described a very foul scent, it was like the scent a man who haven't taken a bath since birth. We don't know who she was or what she wanted since that was the first and the last time we ever saw her.

CHAPTER IX

EMBRACING THE CURSE

In time, my understanding widened. I began to realize that these entities will always be here, be it malignant or not, they are a part of this world. First was the acceptance part, I will always see what others do not, hear what others cannot, feel what others may not, and not all may be able to understand. I will be judged, I will be laughed at, but I will endure. Second, faith and belief that Jesus Christ is more powerful than any entities lurking in this world, and with faith I will always have power over them. Some of them are just lost spirits who need help, while some are just evil spirits feeding on our weaknesses, preying on our fears to inflict pain on our souls.

In time, I began to embrace the gift and used it in helping others...

The Protector- I have a female friend who was in her mid-30s. I knew her because we were both members of a Christian organization for single men and women. She had fair skin, good body figure, attractive looking face, and with a stable job.

For an average guy, she was an ideal woman to marry and build a family. But even with all of her qualities, there was something mysterious about her which was the reason why she never had a boyfriend since birth. No man dared court her, even those that attempted, ended up not talking to her after several dates. At first she questioned herself what was wrong with, then she experienced anxiety, until she eventually recovered and learned to accept it in time.

One night when we went to her apartment for a prayer meeting. It was her first time hosting our prayer meeting so this was also my first time visiting her place. There were about 15 of us. I was seated in the back, right next to the door which opens straight towards the stairs. Doing my best to focus, I tried to close my eyes, but I was confusingly anxious. I feel like there was something in her house that is making me uncomfortable. Something like an entity lurking, not malignant, not evil, it feels like it was just there to protect, no matter what the cost. Since I was sitting right next to the door, everyone who goes in or out inevitably gets my attention. The prayer meeting has not begun, so while everyone was busy talking and catching up with each other. I was investigating the corners of the house with my eyes, trying to locate the source of this inscrutable feeling. A men wearing a white shirt was climbing the stairs, I turned to greet him, thinking he was one of our members. What I saw instead was a male spirit that looked like it was in his mid-20s. It was tall, dark haired, medium built, and fair skinned but does not have a face. He went straight to the wall and then vanished like a bubble disappearing in thin air. I tried to ignore it and focused on our prayer meeting which was now starting. After we sang songs of praises, we always enjoy some snacks provided by the host, which is, the subject of our story. I followed my friend to her kitchen to help her prepare the food. She cautioned me to join the others and that she can handle it. I was persistent since I could not understand why she would deny a gentleman's offer for help. She knows I'm not attracted to her, she's 10 years older than me for Pete's sake. She advised me again not to help and that she was alright but I was stubborn so she finally gave in and let me help.

While she was preparing the bread, she asked me to wash the fruits by the sink. I turned the faucet on, washing the fruits one-by-one when I suddenly noticed a figure of a man standing on my left side, when I turned to face him, he suddenly disappeared. It looked to be the same ghost I saw disappearing through the wall.

I felt a dark depressing feeling inside my heart as the surrounding became cold and heavy which usually is a sign of a spirit in distress lurking around. Suddenly he re-appeared on my right side. This time, he was looking at me ferociously with hateful incriminating eyes. I don't know if it was angry because I was in the kitchen which could be its resting place? Or could it be a jealous entity attracted to my friend? Or maybe it was an over-protective deceased relative.

By this time I was already used to seeing different kinds of apparitions and decided to ignore him. We were all eating by the living room, sharing learnings regarding the bible scripture we read and I almost forgot about the angry spirit by the kitchen. When it was her time to share, I was distracted by a tall shadowy figure standing behind her. It looked like the silhouette of the ghost I saw earlier. It was just there, standing beside her, staring at her, watching over her, like the Queen's guard in London. She noticed how seriously I was staring with a concerned look in my face towards the blank space behind her so she turned to see what I was looking at. Puzzled, for she could not see anything, she then looked me in the eye and asked me if I'm ok with a concerned tone in her voice. I quickly, but unconsciously answered her question with another question,

"Can I use your bathroom?"

I was not sure of what I was about to do, or if what I'm doing was right, or if I even know what I'm doing at all, but I was willing to give it a try. Perplexed with the intent of this specter, I was willing to leave the crowd so as to grant an exclusivity with it to fill know his intentions. I entered the empty bathroom, and sure enough, it didn't take long before an unfavorable presence came to join me.

At first I pretended not to see him while I gather myself to seek some courage from the deep corners of my soul. A deep cold husky voice coming out of its mouth surprised me. No matter how many paranormal beings you see every day, the thrill of an actual encounter still shakes your guts.

"I.... know......... you........ can.......... See.......... Me...."

"Leave.... Her......... alone!!!!!!!"

I froze..

I wanted to talk to him. That's what I came here for. To seek some answer. My knees were terribly shaking, cold drops of sweat raced from my forehead, I wanted to talk but could not find the courage, nor find the right words to say. So I just zipped my pants and went out of the bathroom without washing my hands to rejoin the others. My female friend then asked me "are you okay? You looked like you've seen a ghost?" with concern on her voice. I just answered "I'm ok".

We were about to have our closing prayers. I felt a little guilty not being able to focus on the prayer meeting with all questions in my head that remained unanswered. Is he there to guard my friend or is he there to enslave her? Who is he and how can she get rid of him? Why doesn't he felt like a malignant spirit? These and other questions spiraled through my head until it was time for all of us to go home. I and another friend stayed behind to help her clean out before going home. Nothing out of the ordinary happened while we were tidying up.

We said our goodbyes and went out the door. Before leaving, I took a last look at her apartment. She was standing by the window waving at us. And guess who else was there. Yes! I saw the shadow standing beside her, staring at her, watching over her.

We went out of her gate and I took another last look at her place. On the same exact moment I laid eyes on her apartment was the same exact moment the shadow flew from her window in to my direction, arriving in just a split second to finally confront me face to face before finally screaming.

"LAYAS!!!!!!!!!!!!!!!!!!!!!!!!!"

Which translates "go away" in English.

The following week, we all went on a camping on a mountainous area round north. Everyone was excited about this getaway, having planned this for a long time before it's finally realized. For precautionary measures, we guys decided to take turns in sleeping and assigned a watchmen every hour to watch over the camp while the rest are asleep, we were doing it by pairs. When it was our turn, I might have taken the "watcher thing" a bit too seriously because I was also checking the woods and making sure the tents are secure and all, like a security personnel on patrol.

The night was cold and dark as the moon hid under a blanket of grey heavy clouds. As I passed by my "female friend's" tent, what I saw broke the stillness and silence inside me. Frozen by fear and confusion as I saw the same shadow I saw in her apartment standing beside her tent, staring at her tent.

The sky could no longer contain the water and it started raining heavily leaving the tents all soaked and the ground all wet. Everyone took shelter under the trees evacuating from the tents due to the water rising from the ground. Unknowingly, unluckily at the same time, my female friend was taking shelter in the same tree I was standing in. There was a moment of silence, deciding if talking to her about this shadow would really be the right thing to do. I was also concerned of what this presence might do to her. So I grabbed the opportunity, and finally confronted her about my questions.

I explained to her all the sightings and encounters from her apartment up until that day. I asked her if she ever experienced any unusual or anything paranormal. At first there was hesitation in her part until she finally looked up, and in a sincere and calm voice, she confessed about how she felt his presence, and that it doesn't seem to bother her she felt like it was there to protect her. Her words filled my bucket of questions with answer allowing me to finally realize why this entity attached itself to her. I then asked if her father was still living, and she said no. His father died at a very young age while she was still a kid and his eldest brother swore in his father's death to look after her and protect her all the time. She added that her eldest brother who was very protective of her, died in his mid-20s. She was the youngest in the family which makes her the baby, while his brother was the eldest, so this brother of hers was always looking after her, scaring her suitors away. He died in a motor cycle accident while he was about to fetch her from school, she was so devastated that time. She looked over her shoulders, left to right, as if she was trying to make sure no one else was listening, before she finally confide to me;

"I think my brother's spirit is here. I think he's everywhere I go. Sometimes it creeps me out especially when I'm alone. It's as if I still do not have my freedom to do or say as I wish"

I took a deep breath, before finally advising her that she needs to pay her brother's resting place a visit and talk to him, tell him that she's alright, thank him for all the love and protection, and that he should rest with the Lord now, and that she can take care of herself now and will forever miss him. He will never be able to cross over if she doesn't release him from his promise. The reason why she needed to visit his resting place to do this, it's because the tomb or the grave serves as a linking or a channel for the non-living to perceive our messages clearly.

Several weeks went by, my friend wasn't able to attend our "once a week" prayer meetings. I never texted her nor called her coz it was something she had to take do on her own.

After a month, we finally saw each other again. There's something new about her. She was looking all blooming and bright with a genuine happiness on her face as she happily approached me. We had such a lively conversation, until our topic suddenly switched to her brother, she informed me how she did exactly as I said. The reason why she wasn't able to attend our past meetings was that she was on vacation in her home town. She visited her brother's grave alone. She cried while talking to his brother and pleaded for him to rest. He has been a loving and caring brother, but it is now time to rest under the loving wings of God. She swore she could feel a hand wrapped around her, It wasn't scary, it felt comforting. After which, she felt like a gazillion burden left her heart.

She is now happily married with 2 kids..

Crying Ghost- We were attending a class reunion from our high school. It was good to catch up with everyone and share smiles and laughter, reminiscing our old foolishness. One of our old classmates whom we will call Ben was particularly silent. He would often smile with the funny stories we share but that was that. I could feel a heavy presence towards him. I approached him just for a small chit chat, but when I tapped his back I had a vision of a crying ghost. I was taken a back. Ben noticed it.

"Hey Ben, how are you? You're a bit silent tonight. That's not the Ben we remember"

"Nah, things just been crazy at home since my father died"

"I understand man, his presence still walks your home right?"

"How do you know?"

"Something in your aura gives it away"

After that confrontation, his mood blossomed a bit, like a pinch of hope and excitement charades his face. After the party, Ben invited me to visit their house to see what I can find. Ever since his father died of a car crash, they've been experiencing a lot of unexplainable things. At times they would hear heavy footsteps walking around mid-night when everyone is asleep. They would also hear the sound of a sobbing man echoing around the walls of the house.

One time, his mother woke up early morning to prepare breakfast. It was still dark when she entered the kitchen and that's when she saw the silhouette of her deceased husband sitting in the table. At first she did not trust her sleepy eyes and half-awake brain so she rubbed her eyes and slapped her face only to find that she wasn't dreaming at all. She knows that her husband loved them, so his "hauntings" left them baffled and confused.

The moment I entered the house, a dark cold feeling be filled my heart, swallowing me in to an abyss of sorrow that a tear unknowingly dropped from my eyes. It wasn't malevolent nor was it dangerous, it was a feeling of remorse for an untimely passing of a soul not ready to go.

As I look towards the hallway, studying the corners of the house, I immediately spotted the source of these ominous emotion, floating towards the room. He was wearing white polo shirt with khaki pants and his face looking, clean and peaceful but full of sorrow and sadness. I asked my friend if I can freely walk around their house without uttering a sign that I have already seen his departed father. He gave me the sign of approval and preceded in guiding me around the premise. I immediately moved to where it went and realized that I have entered master's bed room.

The Ghost of their deceased father was just standing their motionless, looking at a family photo by the dresser. I gave it a sharp and steady look, waiting for its next move. It did not disappoint as its right hand slowly and creepily pointed towards the ceiling, while his bones emit a breaking sound with every move. The ceiling was made of woods and there was a square shaped portion which indicates that it might have been opened before.

From a distance, the opening where the ghost was pointing doesn't look obvious, but if you take a closer look you will know that there is a slight space in between the woods. Our quest for answer is about to be satisfied so I asked my friend to grab a chair so we can try to push the square portion open. He pushed it without force and immediately exposed a new expanse which, I presumed, is unknown to the family by the surprised look in their faces. There were documents of different sorts that Ben and her mother found, which raised their curiosities even more. They discovered that his father had set an educational plan for his 2 younger siblings and discovered a passbook for a savings account. His father had always been secretive and silent, did not leave them empty handed after all. Her mother cried and thanked her deceased husband. A mixed feeling of happiness, sadness, and thankfulness showered towards Ben and his other siblings who were also in tears as they hugged each other. I'll be a liar if I tell you I didn't cry.

As much as this was a lovely affair to witness, I had to leave that time since I needed to go to work. Ben thanked me and showed me to the door. Before I left, I took one last look at the house just like I always do with every place before I leave, I saw the ghost of their father by the window waving at me. The expression on his face changed becoming lighter and happier, looking ready to go towards his final destination.

Ben and I met again the following year for another reunion. He told me ever since that day, his father's spirit never visited them again.

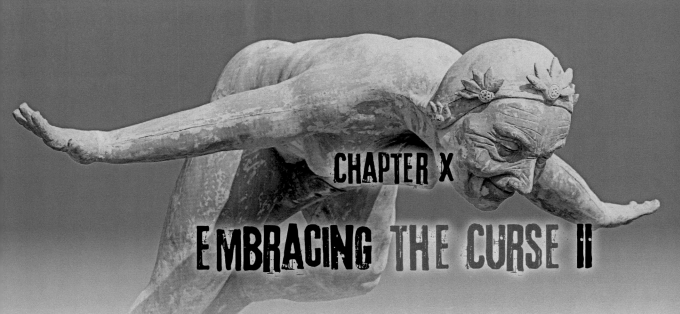

CHAPTER X
EMBRACING THE CURSE II

The Guilt- The devil can take many forms, they can feel your guilt and feed on your sorrows. They will ride on your situation to torment you in any way he can.

Arthur and Martha have always been lovers since college days until they became successful with each other's careers. It didn't take long for the loving couple to be financially stable, soon got married, and bought a home near the city. Determined to be good parents, and given that Arthur's income was sufficient for the entire family, they both decide for her to be a "stay-at-home" mom. When they discovered that she was pregnant, she immediately quit her job so she can take better care for the baby.

Time flew by so fast without everyone noticing, the baby boy was now 11 months old. It grew to be a healthy, loving, and happy baby. As time flew by, Arthur began rendering over times to get extra pay so he can continue supporting his family's growing needs, while Martha unconsciously shifted all her attentions towards the child, creating a growing gap between the couple without them knowing.

One day, Arthur advised Martha that his boss is sending him on a business trip that weekend. This left Martha wondering why he was given such a short notice, for in the past he was always informed at least a week in advance. He said it was last minute instruction from his boss and it was very important. Martha told Arthur that she was very sick and could really use a hand with the baby. Arthur's mind was set and refused to heed the words of his wife, and went on this trip anyway thinking Martha was just being lazy.

Martha, light headed, feverish, with high body temperature, decided to put the baby to sleep in his room, thinking she might feel better if she could just soak herself on a hot bath in the tub. She filled the tub with warm water, but just as she dipped the tub she immediately felt very cold and she was chilling all over. With a dizzy head and blurry visions, she ran towards her bed and wrapped herself with the blanket to warm herself. Having high fever and chills, she finally collapsed under the comfort of her sheets and fell asleep. Somehow the baby woke up and crawled down from his crib climbing over the stuffed animals, crawling his way into his mother's bed room. The baby loved bath time and playing in the water so when he saw that the bathroom door open, he took the opportunity to crawl in the tub.

A cold wind suddenly blew, swinging the bathroom window open and an unknown force in a form of a shadow with deadly intent pushed the innocent child in to the tub. The infant desperately flapping his hand, hopelessly grasping for air as he slowly slip towards his death. It wasn't long for the poor soul to finally lose his life. Martha woke up a few hours later, beating herself and panicking why she felt asleep and left the baby unattended. Taking gigantic and rapid steps, heading towards the baby's room, worried to death about his whereabouts. She almost exploded in fear when she found out that the baby was no longer on his crib. She looked everywhere but could not find the young child is, she was in panic and her hands where uncontrollably shaking as he call Arthur's phone. He didn't pick up. She kept trying anyway as she anxiously check every corner of the house. Arthur noticed his phone ringing but Lennie grabbed it from him and hid it under the blanket.

"No Phones, today you're mine alone", as she continue kissing him.

Martha noticed that the bathroom door was open, the only place in the house she haven't checked yet. With heavy dragging steps, she slowly approached the room, afraid of the vision that may be waiting for her. She was praying for her guts to be wrong. It seemed like eternity before the full view of the tub came in to sight. Nothing could have prepared her for that tragic night when she saw the lifeless baby floating in the tub, motionless, and out cold. She immediately grabbed him trying to check for any signs of life, but there was none, she was shaking all over her body as she desperately tried to revive the child. She rushed him to the nearest hospital but he was long gone.

The baby was dead on Arrival (DOA)..

Martha was consumed with guilt and anxiety. She barely eats and just hides under the cover of her bed, crying all day. Arthur was also filled with guilt, only of he had stayed during that weekend and did not go on a secret weekend getaway with Lennie, the baby would still be alive. He lied, and no one else knew except him and Lennie. He cheated, and now it resulted to the death of his son. He went back to work but was always dysfunctional, his mind floating in the clouds and lost in the thoughts of "what-could-have-been". His boss gave him a time to grieve and advised him to come back when he's ready.

This unfortunate and painful event not only lead to a deeper gap between him and his wife, but this also created a gap between him and Lennie. He wasn't responding to Lennie's calls and messages anymore, blaming the affair between the two of them and their weekend getaway. Paranoia and anxiety drowned her in to a pool of despair, leading to suicidal thoughts. She threatened him that she would kill herself if he continues to ignore her, or he would tell Martha about the two of them, but Arthur filled with grief and guilt ignored her warnings and ignored her constant plea for attention.

One day, Arthur feeling the urge to answer the call of human desires, tried to call Lennie. He tried contacting her through her phone but it was clearly off, so he tried her messenger, but surprisingly, she have not been active for several days now. Puzzled by this circumstance, Arthur decided to go to her apartment directly. The door locked with a police seal blocking the door. This left Arthur in to an ocean of questions. He went around asking the neighbors. Nothing could have prepared her for the shock of his life when, for was informed by the bystanders that she committed suicide a couple of days ago by hanging herself.

Arthur never attended her memorial nor the funeral. He wept silently. First was his son, and now his concubine, could this be the punishment for all the wrong he did? Alternatively, could this be a mean to bury the secret along with her grave and start anew?

One night, Martha was crying under her pillows when she heard the cry of a baby coming from her son's room. She stopped, listened, she swore she could her son crying. Filled with vast longing, Martha came running in to her baby's room.

"Mommy's coming baby!!"

Her crying heart was not disappointed, for there he was, in his crib, laying, gently weeping, and begging for a touch of affection. She picked her up and held him in her loving arms. *"oh God! My baby"* filled with so much love and excitement as she cradle him in her arms.

Arthur also came in the room to check the commotion. Her excited eyes met his confused face, proud of the bundle of joy in her arms

"Arthur, look! Our son is alive!"

Arthur looking at her wife, heart filled with remorse and pity, cradling their son's stuffed animal in her arms, delicately tucking it under the warmth of her breast, heart fully convinced that it was her son in her arms. Tears escaped from his eyes, blaming himself for the demise of their only son and the deterioration of his wife's sanity. Yes, things are falling apart for Arthur. He took slow and heavy steps as he make his way towards her. Somehow he has to break her heart and wake her up to the truth.

"I'm sorry Martha, our son is dead!"

"Don't you dare say that! Can't you see? He is very much alive!"

"No Martha!" he didn't finish, Martha slapped him in the face.

"Don't you see?" Arthur broke down and grabbed the stuffed animal, it was only then that Martha realized that it wasn't real. Her fantasy has been broken, violently shaken back to the painful truth that their son, their loving boy was no more. She broke down and cried and so did Arthur.

Martha cried until she fell asleep on the floor. She was still hugging the stuffed animal in her arms. Arthur just stood there tearfully watching her wife. He felt so much pity for her, he couldn't believe what happened to their happy marriage. What happened to their family? If only he didn't cheat with Lennie, who knows, their son would have been alive, she would have been alive, and his wife wouldn't be in this pitiful situation.

"Arthur"

A cold voice hushed in his ear...

"Arthur!"

The voice sounded like it was in deep agony and pain. This unknown voice could have shaken the hell out of him except that there was something about it that was very familiar. It can't be possible. No, it can't be real. Arthur thought that he might just be hallucinating, trying to make sense of the unthinkable truth.

"Arthur!!!!"

"huhuhu!!!!"

This time, it wasn't just calling out his name, it was also crying. The voice sounded so cold and heavy, as if it was piercing right through his soul. He gathered his courage and followed the voice, which seemed to have come from the kitchen. When he reached the kitchen, he couldn't believe what he was seeing! It was Lennie, sitting in a pool of blood! Her blood! Her lifeless face was dead pale, sorrow and mourn filled her eyes, kitchen knife on her left hand while the right hand wrist was cut open creating an escape passage of the blood from her body to the floor. With dismay and pity in his voice, the only words that came out of his mouth was;

"Oh Lennie, what have you done to yourself?"

Terror reigned his heart when the lifeless body started to move started speaking...

"Arthur! Help me!!"

Arthur!!!!

AaaAAArthurRrrrr!!!!!!!!!!!

The dreaded figure sounded more and more aggravated every time it calls his name without getting any response. Mixed emotions clouded his judgements, consternation and pity, battling in his mind before finally dropping to the floor, weeping...

Enough!!!! Enough!!!!

Arthur broke down, tears and mucus dripping from his face. He whimpered,

I'm sorry Lennie!!!

I'm sorry son!!!

I'm sorry Martha!!!

Just when he thought the peak of the fright is over, the sound of broken bones crisply cracking filled the room as Lennie crawled her way towards Arthur. She crawled slowly, as if it could barely carry itself. Blood trail followed its path while its left hand dragged the knife along. The motive of this approaching horror was clear; it was determined to carry out its insidious plan of taking Arthur with her. In a low and cold voice, the spirit spoke...

"Arthur! Held me Arthur!!! I Feel so alone."

"Follow me baby!" come with me, me and your son! Let's be a family"*

Arthur just sat there crying... weeping... unable to move, while Lennie's spirit finally reached him, handing him the knife she was carrying.

"Here Arthur, Here's the knife! We'll be together forever!"

"Just the 3 of us!! We'll be a happy family"

Arthur! AARTHURRR!!!!!!!!!

AAAaarturRrrRRRRRR!!!!!!!!!!

The sprit is not simply pleading but the voice became angry and demanding.

"If you won't follow me, I will take you!! I will drag your filthy wife along to the caverns of hell!!!

"YOU WILL DIE!!!! YOU WILL ALL DIE!!!!!!!!!!!!!!!"

GRAAAAAAaaaaAAAAAAA!!!!!!!!!!!!!!!!!!!!!!!!!

"God! What have I done?"

Arthur wept.

The once weak and dying spirit was now rising from the floor. Grudge filled her broken soul with courage as she slowly lifted the sharp object in the air, dead-set on sticking it in to his heart. Arthur closed his eyes just waiting for the metal to reach his heart and take away his pain. He finally passed out; he was awaken by the beam of the sun, escaping through the window curtains, making its way in to his eyes. The apparition was no longer there when he woke up; he would have successfully convinced himself that everything was just a nightmare, except that the knife was still laying coldly in his hand. Everything else vanished like a bubble blowing in the air, no blood, no Lennie, no nothing!

Everything seemed normal that day. Arthur and Martha went to visit their son's grave. They planned to stay till late in the afternoon. They brought along, snacks, food, water, sodas, and a huge umbrella all packed to spend the whole day in the cemetery. They just want a quiet time away from the living world, a quality time with their son, and with each other. They just enjoyed each other's company. Sitting beside their son's grave. Resting under the shade of a tree, enjoying the cold breeze of the wind blowing through the leaves. Arthur could not help but look back on the horror that happened, or might have imagined the night before. Pressed by guilt and remorse, he was so tempted to tell his wife about Lennie but he was not ready to face the possibility of the consequences that may result from this revelation. He battled against himself and finally concluded that this may not be the right time to tell his wife about his affair with Lennie. While he was lost in deep thoughts, his wife was looking at her mobile phone going over the photos of their son from when he was still alive.

"Arthur!"

"Arthur!"

Arthur heard a faint voice that sounded almost like a whisper carried by the wind. He looked towards Martha's face trying to see what her reaction was, but there was no sign of her hearing the questionable sound. He turned around to see where it was coming from. From a distance, he saw a familiar figure wearing a long white dress covered in blood. He tried to ignore it, as if he did not see it. Unfortunately, which ever direction he looks, the lady seemed to be there, it's like a stain in his eyes that refuses to go away. Afraid of anything worse to follow, he advised his wife that it was getting dark and they should probably go home now. Martha who was comfortable sitting and enjoying the moment was baffled, her mood suddenly changed, she became hysterical and started crying. The calmness in her face was replaces with insanity and anxiety.

"No Arthur, I can't leave our son! What if he wakes up and we're not here?"

Arthur could see in his peripheral view, how the figure was getting closer and closer by the moment. Dark heavy cloud filled the sky, and the surrounding suddenly went dark. It was still 4 in the afternoon but the dark blanket of grey cloud covering the sky is making it seem like it was night time. Cold breeze blew from the east while Martha was just sitting their crying. Sobbing... Arthur could feel panic starting to raise inside of him while Martha remains inconsolable..

"No Arthur!"

"We can't leave"

"You can't leave me!!!"

"Not AGAIN!!!"

Martha's voice became loud and demonic, echoing from all directions while her hair is being harassed by the wind blowing all over the place. Arthur has never been so afraid in his entire life. Her voice sounded like thunder.

"Martha what are you talking about?"

He grabbed her by the hand but she pushed him away, causing him to fall down to the ground. Her face came in to view, only then did he realized that the lady beside her was no longer his wife but is Lennie. Her hair suddenly became frizzy, face as pale as white, deep evil eyes with no eyeballs piercing straight in to his soul, hate and anger was very visible in her dead face, like it was eating him. She screamed and a swarm of insects came out of her mouth like a tornado attacking Arthur. He tried to shake them away but there were too many of it all over the place. He stood up and sprinted towards his car barely seeing anything. His foot got entangled with a rock causing him to fall and crash into a tomb stone. Nothing could have prepared him when he came face to face with the photo of the person buried in that grave, it was Lennie's grave! He froze in fear. Suddenly, a hand creeped its way out of the grave and grabbed his foot, it was the cold hand of a decaying corps escaping from 6 feet below, with one purpose. That is, to drag him with her to hell. It was the most disgusting thing he's ever seen in his life, the skin peeling from its fingers exposing the bones with worms and insects crawling from inside out. And the smell, the smell of rotting flesh is just so foul that he finally threw up. No matter how hard he struggled, the ground was eating him until he couldn't see anything anymore. Too dark, he couldn't breathe, he was completely swallowed by the ground.

"Arthur!" Wake up!"

Arthur was breathing heavily with sweats all over his body. He kissed his wife. It was all a nightmare. He invited his wife to start heading home to which she complied. When he stood up, he almost fell and lost his footing. There was a swell in his foot shaped like a hand.

When they arrived home, Martha went straight to bed. He sat by the living room for a second then decided to head out. He couldn't take it anymore. He was going crazy. He drove to a friend's house for some company. He need to share this to someone otherwise his head was going to explode.

I heard a knock on my door. It was Arthur.

"Hey Brother!" How are you? It's been such a long time.

The moment I opened the door, I suddenly sensed a dark aura coming from him. He looked restless, tired, and burdened. I was looking at a completely different Arthur, he looked like he was in his sixties. There was an insidious shadow riding over his back. I pretended like I didn't see it. These things don't like to be seen. I came out of the door instead of inviting him inside. I just had a hint of what was happening. If I invite him in, this would invite the devil too. We came to a nearby store and grabbed a beer. First it was small chit chats, catching up, how he and Martha are holding on. When we finished a bottle or two that's when he started to open up. I could barely make up what he was saying since he was crying a lot. I had to ask probing questions to understand.

He told me everything that had happened and I just knew what this is. This is Demonic Oppression. Although we were a little tipsy over the bottles of beer, I just knew that this could not and should not wait till morning. I had a friend who was a priest living in a seminary house in the downtown area. It was only a 10 to 15 minute drive.

I immediately took him to the priest and we arrived around 11 pm hoping he was still awake. We go stocked in the guard house. He wouldn't let us in. I told him to please call Fr. Reyes and that it was an emergency. Moments later Fr. Reyes came in to full view and invited us in. I couldn't believe the look on his face when he saw Arthur. I bet he could see the devil ridding in his back too. He motioned for us to go the chapel. He and Arthur needed some space so he can confess his sins and he can pray for him. While they were speaking with each other heart-to-heart, I was there in the back praying intervention. The devil wasn't able to enter the chapel. I looked through the windows and there in the darkness it lurked.

Its eyes looked at me with extreme anger. It was breathing heavily. Its eyes were fiery red. Its horn and fangs were very sharp. Its skin was very dark. Slowly it lifted his hand and I could see that it was holding someone by the neck. I couldn't make out the face, but it looked like a silhouette of a woman. The devil then ran his finger across his neck. It was a signal. It was going to kill. But who? Oh God!

"Arthur! Who's with Martha?"

"I left her alone" answered Arthur

"Fr. Reyes, we have to leave. We have to leave now. Please come with us father"

Fr. Reyes must have understood the urgency by the looks in my eyes and the sound of my voice. Arthur kept asking,

"What's happening? What's going on?"

"Arthur, its Martha. We need to go to your house now, and we need to do it fast"

Meanwhile, Martha woke up in middle of the night to the sound of a baby crying. There it was again, instead of being afraid she was delighted. In her heart it was her lost son's spirit visiting her. She rushed to her dead son's room.

"Mommy's coming baby!"

Her heart was filled with excitement her soul was filled with hope.

"Mommy's coming baby!"

Tears racing down from her eyes. These are tears of Joy.

"Mommy's coming baby!"

Longing to caress him close to his heart again.

"Mommy's coming baby!"

She swung the door wide open and rushed in to the bed of the crying baby. There he was laying there with his cute nose, teary eyes, and chubby rosy cheeks. Martha rushed to pick him up but when she held him close to her heart the baby became a stuffed animal again. She dropped it to the floor.

She heard the baby crying again, this time, it was coming from her bed room. Martha sprinted to go back to her room, she stopped by the bedroom door when the bathroom door swung open exposing a thick fog inside. When the fog started to clear, she could hear a splashing sound by the tub so she went in and saw that it was her baby drowning. She tried to enter the bathroom but an unforeseen force blocked her from entering. She felt helpless, she was just looking at her baby drowning. As if the devil was toying with her and just wanted her to suffer, helplessly witnessing her baby slowly drowning.

Martha was hysterically screaming trying to break free to save her baby. The invisible force suddenly disappeared and Martha fell in to the tub. She tried to search for the baby. She was splashing around the tub trying to find the drowning child but with no luck. Just then, she had a glimpse of a child running out of the door. She followed the drops of water by the floor going in to the baby's bedroom.

The moment she entered the baby's room, the door behind her suddenly slammed shut. All windows suddenly swung open and strong wind entered the room blowing the curtains away. Due to the strength of the wind the curtain ripped and started to take the form of a white lady holding a child. Martha dropped to the floor crying. She doesn't understand what was going on. The apparition started walking towards the baby's bed to pick up the child which was in bed now. Martha felt a strong rage firing inside her, burning all of her fears away.

"NO YOU DON'T!!!"

"YOU DON'T TAKE MY BABY AWAY FROM ME!!!!"

She lunged into the figure which was slowly disappearing in the open window. She tried to grab it but all she got was a curtain. She lost her footing and the curtain circled around her neck strangling her. She tried to regain her balance but she couldn't. She was wet and her feet were slippery. She was choking, dying, her vision slowly blurring. Her eyes caught the glimpse of a red giant figure standing in the corner of the room. With long horns and pointy ears, it was watching her, laughing at her struggle. She was blacking out and the last thing she remembered was the door swinging open.

Fr. Reyes and Arthur rushed in to help Martha but I got held back by the figure I saw lurking in the corner of the room. This insidious presence clearly is the one tormenting this house. Martha and Arthur reunited and she was slowly getting her consciousness back. I called father and pointed my eyes towards the figure by the corner. Fr. Reyes saw it and armed herself with the crucifix and holy water from his pocket.

"In The Name of the Father"

"And of the Son"

"And of the Holy Spirit!"

Strong wind blew from the window and we were blown into the wall. Fr. Reyes picked himself up and preceded with his prayers.

"With the authority given to me by the Holy Spirit!!!"

"Depart devil in the Name of Jesus Christ!!!!"

"Leave this family and take your filt with you!!!!"

Things were flying from every direction, doors and windows were swinging, It was as if a hurricane was happening inside the room. My legs were shaking with fear. Everything seem blurry with the lights flickering on and off and all the things flying around. It shames me to admit that during that time fear overcame me and it felt as if I was faithless towards the Lord.

The last thing I heard was Fr. Reyes's strong scream. And just like what you see in the movies, everything went to a stop. I knew Fr. Reyes defeated the devil. The light stopped flickering, the wind stopped blowing, and the doors and windows stopped swinging. The room was all messy and full of sheets and broken glasses. Martha picked up a photo of their son that fell from the wall. She cried as she cleaned the frame with her wrist. Fr. Reyes, approached her..

"It was not your son. It was never your son. The devil walks within us and attacks us where we are most weak."

They are the kings of deceit and can take the forms to adjust to our fears, our guilt, and traumas and attack our soul"

The couple went into confession. Arthur told Martha everything. After several counseling and seminars, the couple was able to work on their marriage. They left and move to a different city to start over. We still keep in touch from time-to-time. They now have 3 children and are active with charity and church activities.

CHAPTER XI

NEW HOME

After we left the ancestral house, we rented a small apartment that wasn't far from where we used to live. It wasn't such a good neighborhood to say the least, but it was all we could afford back then. There were police bust from time-to-time due to drug related cases and illegal gambling. The apartment we were renting was a 2 story house with 2 rooms. According to the owner, it's been vacant for quite some time now.

When we moved in, I could feel a heavy presence. Like an evil entity was lurking in the midst. Maybe it was just the feeling of moving to a small house from a huge one that dictates this emotion. Well, I should have trusted my instincts.

At first, there were minor occurrences. Furniture rearranged the next day, the Crucifix would be missing from the altar and would be found under the chair, and doors would open and close by itself.

From there it was starting to get worst. There was a sudden decline of health particularly with my mother. She began to lose weight and developed a strong cough. We took her to the doctors and everything was ok. The environment may have been challenging in terms of the people but the area was clean.

One night, I woke up and went to the bathroom to take a leak. When I passed by my parent's room, I saw a black figure floating in the air that entered their room through the wall.

Based on experience, black hooded entities are always evil so I knocked on my parent's room.

No one was answering, I know they were already asleep but I have to wake them up. I could hear noise from inside their room. I was no longer knocking but banging the door. Moments later my father opened the door and I saw my mom sitting in her side of the bed trying to catch her breath. I could see panic on her face and the look of confusion on my father's face. I asked my mom if she was alright and she informed me that she was having a nightmare. She told me that a figure of a black woman entered their room through the wall and went straight towards her, strangling her. She tried to break free but the entity was very strong. She tried to wake my father but no voice came out of her mouth and her entire body could not move. She was able to break free when my father woke up due to the loud banging on the door. Now I was able to confirm that an evil spirit lives within these walls. But why just show herself now? Why all so sudden? This spirit was evil, and this is malevolent. I need to do something. .

I was using the bathroom and I noticed a black figure standing in the corner from my peripheral vision. This time, I was strong in faith. And I rebuked this spirit.

"In the Name of the Lord Jesus Christ!, depart from me you evil spirit!"

And it was gone.

On a separate incident, I was sweeping the floor and whichever directions I face, this figure was there trying to bother me. If this would have happened to a different person they would have ran for their lives. But not me, I am stronger now. So I rebuked it again and it just disappeared.

On this particular night, the entity decided to show its face to me. I was washing the dished. In front of our sink was a mirror which faces directly towards the living room. My mother was watching a television with a sad look on her face. She watching the Good Friday dramas. It is customary here in the Philippines that during the Lenten season, television networks would show short drama films. I would look at my mother's face occasionally through the mirror. I was having fun with her facial expressions getting carried away by the drama and all. I dropped one of the glasses I was holding in the sink, good thing it didn't break. When I looked in to the mirror again.

I saw the black lady apparition. She was standing right behind me, looking at me through the mirror. She was wearing a black veil that matched her black outfit. Her eyes were so red that it looked like it was glowing. Her left hand slowly moved until it pointed towards my mother.

That got me raging mad. I rebuked the spirit. This time I was more determined to not just rebuke it but to cast it away. I asked my mother to go to confession the next day. From then on I invited my brothers in church every week to spend our prayer meetings at home. When No one was watching TV, I made sure that the Christian praise songs are playing in the living room.

That black lady never dared show its self again until one night. My mother was about to go bed so she turned off all the lights from downstairs. When she reached the last flight a hand grabbed her leg and dragged her in to the darkness downstairs. My mom was screaming hysterically and it woke me up. I quickly stood up from my bed to help my mom but the door in my room suddenly shut close missing my nose by an inch. My mom was still screaming downstairs but this time she sounded like she was choking. I had to break the window glass and climb down since the door would not open. When I opened the door, my mom was down in the floor laying. On top of her was the black lady choking her. I ran to her rescue but a chair came flying hitting me in the head. Black lady really are powerful entities. My head was throbbing in pain so I was slowly crawling towards my mother. When I was right under the table, the knife fell towards me but I was able to dodge it. I tried to grab my mother but I was only able to grab her bracelet and it broke. When the bracelet broke, the black lady let out a scream and let go of my mom. She was able to break free and was now catching her breath. The black lady slowly turned, shifting her attention to me. It gave me an insidious look full of anger and of hate! It was preparing to attack me. I was getting ready for the worst part, I just told myself, "at least mom is safe now".

Out of nowhere, a small light caught my attention on my right side. It was the altar. I noticed that the black lady was now floating in the air and was about to attack me. Her hands getting ready to strangle me to death. I didn't know what to do anymore so I picked up the crucifix and wrapped the broken bracelet around it.

The black lady let out a very horrible scream before it disappeared like a bubble in the thin air. I looked at the bracelet; it was a 14-karat gold with black pearl beads. I asked my mom where she got it from, she said she found it when we moved in and forgot to tell us about it. I wrapped the bracelet around the crucifix and sealed it. I dug a hole in the ground right next to the house and buried it there to make sure no one would find it ever again. I left a stone on its midst to mark its location. I don't know why I did that, I just thought I should.

Years later, I happened to have visited that place where I buried it and checked if it was still there. That specific spot where I hid that tiny piece of horror was dug. The stone was no longer there. A chill of terror ran down my spine as I dug the hole to make sure it's still there. It's gone! Somebody must have found it. God bless his soul!

CHAPTER XII

EMBRACING THE CURSE III

Exorcism- James looked at his watch again. It was now 10 pm.

The coast was clear and the night was still. He can no longer hear the sound of footsteps lurking in the house, nor any voice speaking. The television off and the lights are out signifying that everyone is now asleep. James slowly opened his door and it let out a soft squeak.

Pause

He peeked through the door before opening the door another inch.

Pause

His head can now fit through the door opening and he looked through the left, and then looked through the right. This is it. He grabbed his bag and his shoes as he cautiously tiptoed out of his room. He slowly closed the door behind him. He passed by his parents room and he could hear them from the closed door. He paused for a while. They are praying the rosary. Good sign. After they pray the rosary, they would then go to sleep after.

He finally reached the doorway. He can't go through the door. Opening it would create too many noises with all the locks there are. He went to his usual exit point, which is the window by the living room. Their house was a bungalow type so jumping from the window was not a problem. He was finally out and a sense of freedom boiled inside him. He grabbed his bike, wiped the cold sweat dripping from his forehead and started walking towards the gate. On his right, a glimpse of light caught his attention. It was coming from the grotto that is shedding light to the image of the Virgin Mary. He looked at it with hate and despair, before proceeding with his escape plan. He wasn't running away, he just couldn't tell his parents where he was going. They are very religious and it would be such a controversy if they know what he is involved with.

Years ago, he was not doing any of the stuffs he is doing now, nor was he involved with any of the gangs he affiliated with right now.

Years ago, he was once a religious and faithful boy who abide by his parent's word. However, he wasn't smart in the head, even with his efforts of studying he was still failing in his Math class. He begged the teacher for a special project but she never listened, he prayed in the church daily but to no avail. He still failed. During the time when he was so down and broken hearted, he found his way through the most unsavory type of individuals. They were the ones who led him to the trouble he is in right now, a life full of concealment and secrecy. Since then, he became mischievous, rebellious, and secretive. The boy that brought so much happiness to his parents has now become a headache.

He soon arrived in their meeting place.

A museleo (*1 : a large tomb especially : a usually stone building with places for entombment of the dead above ground- Merriam's English Dictionary*) in the most secluded part of the abandoned cemetery.

Dark and misty was the night, if it wasn't for the few candles and the light coming from the cigarettes smoked by the gang they'd be in complete darkness. As he came closer and closer, the familiar smell began to fill the air. Smell of fresh blood coming from the goat and cigarette smoke feels like music to his heart. It was ritual night and all members gathered to worship their god, evil god. He parked his bicycle on an old tomb. He noticed a statue of an angel standing above it with its right hand extended as if it was raising something. He hang his bag by the statue's hand and he took out his cape, wore it and joined the others. They were all surrounding a tomb inside the museleo and on top of the tomb was a drawing of a pentagram with candles in each corner. The head of the dead goat placed in the middle of the pentagram with blood poured over it. The leader commanded the members to bring in the sacrifice. It was a poor teenage girl the gang kidnapped, mouth covered with tape and hands tied together. They were carrying her since she was unconscious while her foot was dragged across the floor. They stripped her clothes off and layed her down in the cold blood-spilled floor. The leader was going to have sex with her before killing her. She remains unconscious, or at least I think she is, as a tear run down her rosy innocent looking face. James felt a pain in his heart. It's been too long since he feel pity nor remorse in his cold heart. He wish there was something he could do. What was he thinking?

This is supposed to be an evil ritual! There's no room for pity here. The leader was starting to remove his garment and James couldn't bear to see the sight. As he closed his eyes shut, one of the candle light died causing a distraction. The leader turned towards James, he knew it was him that caused the distraction. He was feeling pity towards the girl and this is not satan's way that's why the connection broke.

The leader was slowly walking towards him with a knife in his hand. Cold sweat ran down his head. He was looking at the other members but their faces remain colored with blank emotions. No one was going to save him from the wrath of the leader. He was now a foot away when a smoke grenade suddenly landed near his feet. Suddenly, police officers entered the scene and everyone was scrambling. It was a total chaos, screaming, yelling, smoke, and lights from different directions. There was total tranquility as the police tried to arrest as many as they can and people desperately tried to flee from the scene. James was able to run from the scene by crawling through the floor. He was stomped upon and stepped on but it didn't matter, the sudden rush of adrenaline was enough for him to be numb from the pain. He got his bag and his bike and slowly crawled his was in to the empty woods when suddenly, someone grabbed him from behind. It was their leader! He grabbed his bag and stuffed the goat head and the sharp knife inside.

"Take it! And keep it safe!"

James fled from the scene through the woods. Good thing the police never followed him there. He was still shaking when he got home. He didn't care whether his parents would hear him or not. Fear and adrenaline still running through his veins and all he wanted to do was to hide behind the covers of his blanket. He rushed towards his room leaving a trail of dirty footprints and blood, dripping from his bag due to the goat head stuffed in there by the cult leader.

He entered his room, opened his closet doors and threw the bag before crashing in to his cozy bed. With the rush of blood pumping through his veins, creating a pulse in his head, it was almost difficult to sleep. Turning from side-to-side, going over the things that have happened, thinking how he could have ended in jail or something. He stood up, opened his closet and got his bag. The stench of dying animal escaped through the air as he uncover the goats head, kissed it, and hanged it together with his clothes. A feeling of relief reigned in his heart and soon he was able to sleep.

"Lando!!!"

"There's blood and mud all over the floor coming from the window towards James' room!!!"

"Shut up Linda! Relax, nothing's wrong with him. I mean physically his ok"

"What do you mean his ok?"

"I woke up in the middle of the night and went to the kitchen for a glass of water and I saw him walking towards his room"

"Was he hurt?"

"Where did he go?"

"Did you ask him where he went?"

"He's ok believe me, but we need to talk to him about this behavior"

The couple agreed, it's been a while since the last time they talked to their son. He's been so distant and silent lately. They knocked in his door but there was no response.

"Tok tok tok"

"James?"

"tok tok tok"

"James?"

He grabbed the doorknob and twisted it, it wasn't locked. He slowly pushed the door open and a foul smell filled the entire room, causing the couple's eyebrows to meet and their hearts to pound. It smelled like somebody died in there. James might be a hard headed kid but they know he wouldn't go as far as killing someone. There was no sign of James so they ventured in to the room and checked where the smell was coming from.

The windows were covered with black curtains that no light from the sun can get in. As they turned on the light, darkness still reigned due to the red film covering the bulb. His father noticed the posters in the wall, due to the darkness he needed to take a closer look. What he discovered shook the sanity out him when he realized that the entire room was filled with posters and drawings of Satan and devils. His heart pounded so much that he could barely breathe like he was gonna have a heart attack, so he ran for the windows and forcefully removed the black curtain. Sun light finally entered the room exposing the dark secrets hidden by James. Posters of Baphomet covered the walls, goat hooves tied to ropes decorated the ceiling, and demonic drawings on the wall that looked like they were drawn using blood. Linda, could not take what she was looking at and she dropped to the floor and vomited. With teary eye, Lando approached the dresser and opened the drawer. Knives, bloody silverwares, and upside down crosses caught his attention. He ventured deeper in to his son's secrets. They might be wrong about their son after all, he's gotten worst.

Following the stench that seemed to be coming from the closet, he dragged his feet, too afraid of what he might see. He made the sign of the cross, and slowly placed his hand in the closet door knob. Anxious about what he might discover inside, too afraid thinking a dead body could be there. His sweaty hand pulled the door open and an even fouler smell escaped through the air along with the swarm of flies buzzing all around. Lando saw a pair of red eyes peeked from under the closet. Soon a set of white teeth with fangs joined the pair of red eyes. The evil smile caused Lando's hair to stand and a strong fear overpowered him. They came out of his room running for their lives..They haven't seen James that entire day, so they waited the next day to confront him. James was still feeling pretty banged up from last night. It was already 9 am and he haven't eaten his breakfast yet. He opened the front door and discovered his parents were waiting for him in the living room. Linda's eyes were red and teary, looking at his boy, his son, wondering what has happened to him over the years.

Argument aroused between James and his parents, hurtful words and languages came out of his mouth. Lando was taken aback causing him to slap him in the face. James became aggravated and pushed Lando throwing him several feet away before finally landing in the couch. He was very strong! He ran and locked himself in his room.

"James!!!"

"Leave him alone Linda!"

"Leave him alone"

Baffled at the actions of their son, the couple was left crying.

The next morning was a beautiful Sunday...The parents planned to take James to a Christian gathering in a popular mall. However, there was a problem, how do they get him to go with them? Well, the gathering was in a mall. They can take him for shopping and will not mention the gathering.

"Hey son"

"I was wondering.. well, we were wondering if you want to go to the mall with us for a little shopping"

"It's been a while since we all went out,
What do you say? You get dressed up?"
James was hesitant but realized he need a new black curtain to replace the ones his parents tore.
"Do I get to choose whatever I want to buy?"
"Yes!"
"ok then, let's go!"

The entrance to the activity was located right next to the mall's elevator, being one of the supervising committee to the activity; I was responsible of the registration by the entrance. Something caught my attention; it was as if a dark presence was slowly approaching. Looking in each direction trying to locate where this negative aura was coming from. It seemed to be coming from the elevator. I then saw Lando and Linda approaching with their son. That explains this negative feeling, for what was with them was an insidious horror attached to their son, dwelling in his back like a parasite. The way it held on to James indicated that he is the one who owns him and would not let him go without a fight. It wasn't long for James to realize that his parents tricked him in to attending this activity. He started arguing with them,

"YOU LIED TO ME!!!"
"Come on son. It's ok, we'll just drop by and be on our way"
Lando held on to his son's hand but he threw him away.
"Get away from me you worthless son of a bitch!!!!"
James' screamed in a howling deep voice signifying a different entity speaking in his behalf. People started to gather to check what the commotion was all about so Linda was quick to whisper to his son's ear;
"Son, let's not make a scene here. If you don't want to then let's just turn around"
James' face turned to Linda and pushed him saying,
"You deceitful whore!!! You kneel and serve your god when you couldn't even take care of your own son. You failure of a mother!!"
A tear dropped in Linda's face while Lando exploded and punched him in the face. He dropped to the floor and his mother tried to pick him up. A larger crowed now gathered and this time it has caught the attention of Fr. Reyes. He looked at me and I looked at him. With the familiar looks in my face, Fr. Reyes understood what this is, this was the same look I gave him when I took Arthur to him. Lando feeling sorry for his son, regretfully picked him up.
"I'm sorry son"
James was still lying flat in the floor when his head suddenly turned three hundred sixty degrees to face them. Sometimes it got me thinking what happened to his bones and spinal cords.

His eyeballs were gone and it was just all white with red veins. He suddenly screamed so loud, swarm of insects coming out of his mouth, spreading panic and chaos across the place. Fr. Reyes motioned for James to be taken inside the event area but he threw away everyone that have tried to come near him. Yes, he was that strong. With every strike of his arms, no matter how big the person is would eventually be thrown a couple of feet away. His body was terribly shaking while he lay on the floor grunting and screaming. I took the rosary from my bag and made the sign of the Cross, slowly walked towards James and waited for the proper timing. He was moving a lot, it was hard for me to put it on him. Grunting, screaming, with contorted face that seem to be in a state of pain. He tilted his head backward and his body wide stretched. I've been waiting for this opportunity so I instantly ceased it.

In a split of a second, I was able to put the rosary in to his neck. His face still contorted in agonizing pain and his entire body stiffed. He raised his hand and in a deep horrifying voice he screamed,
"Help Me Satan!!!!"
James became motionless and hard as a rock. He wasn't moving anymore, nor can he be moved, it doesn't look like he was breathing. Linda started crying and was becoming hysterical while Lando just stood there motionless not knowing what to do. Too many attentions drawn so we carried James inside and lay him down

in front of the altar we made. Fr. Reyes kissed his robe before putting it on, took out his holy water and crucifix, and prepares to do an exorcism.

"Hush now Linda and Lando, we are going to get him back"

Fr. Reyes made the sign of the cross. Sprinkled holy water on all of us. Then sprinkled holy water on James. Just as the water touched James' cheek it smoked causing him to wake up, screaming in agonizing pain. Fr. Reyes instructed me to repeat after him

"Lord, have mercy."

"Christ, have mercy"

"Lord, have mercy."

"Christ, graciously hear us."

BRAAWWRRRRAWRRRR!!!!!!!!!!!!!!!

James was turning from side-to-side, throwing everything in his path. He was so strong that we could not contain him. There were at least 8 of us straining him, trying to hold him down, but at times he was still able to break free and would often levitate.

Honestly, I could barely focus on the prayer. It's like everything was happening so fast, I did not even notice the mall security personnel entering the venue. I had a glimpse of their faces; they just stood there watching with their jaws dropped.

Fr. Reyes placed the cross in to the forehead of James and it looked like it was burning. Then his entire body was violently shaking and vibrating.

"God, whose nature is ever merciful and forgiving, accept our prayer that this servant of yours, bound by the fetters of sin, may be pardoned by your loving kindness."

"Holy Lord, almighty Father, everlasting God and Father of our Lord Jesus Christ, who once and for all consigned that fallen and apostate tyrant to the flames of hell, who sent your only-begotten Son into the world to crush that roaring lion; hasten to our call for help and snatch from ruination and from the clutches of the noonday devil this human being made in your image and likeness."

The next thing I felt was a green warm jelly-like substance emitted from James' mouth, flowing like a fountain, showering us with this disgusting horror. Fr. Reyes sat on top of James' tommy. He gave him the strongest slap I have ever seen in my entire life, before he grabbed his jaw restricting any further movements.

"WHO ARE YOU DEMON!!!!!!!!!!!!!!!!!!!!!!!"

BRAAWWRRRRAWRRRR!!!!!!!!!!!!!!!

"IN THE NAME OF JESUS! TELL ME YOUR NAME DEMON!!!!!!!!!!!!!"

The next thing I remembered was flying across the room before hitting my head against the wall. I, along with Fr. Reyes and 3 other people were thrown by James in his struggle to break free. I picked up Fr. Reyes and got him back on his feet. His eyes filled with motivation and assertiveness, not willing to give up nor surrender against this malevolent demon, he picked up his cross again and wiped the sweat from his forehead. He sprayed James with the holy water again and he screamed in agonizing pain. Distracted, he didn't see him coming, plunging the crucifix right in to his head. He dropped to the floor once more, screaming even more, eyeball disappeared, face contorted and horrific scream that sounded like it came from the deeps of hell.

"I command you demon. Tell me your name!"

James was violently shaking before finally collapsing. Linda dropped to the floor just as Mary dropped when he saw Jesus Christ hanging on the cross. Her eyes filled with tears, regrets, and questions. What have they done for them to experience this nightmare? She was looking straight towards James' face while her husband was wrapping his hand around her. A tear escaped from James' eye. She knew he's in there, inside, fighting, struggling to break free from the captivity of this devil. His eyes opened and she looked at Linda with pitiful eyes, his face was begging for her help, desperately needing her motherly touch.

"Mom, help me"

"they're hurting me"

"Please tell them to stop"

"My SON! LET GO OF HIM!!!"

"CAN"T YOU SEE? HIS IN PAIN! HE NEEDS ME!"

"Do not be deceived sister! Get a hold of yourself!"

"The devil is tricky and deceiving, do not fall towards his tricks"

Linda believed the priest and shrugged of her husband. Crawling her way towards James, screaming as tears fall from her eyes.

"You get out of his body! You get out right now! You give me my son back!!!"

James' face changed, his eyeballs have disappeared again, and with an insidious voice, he screamed;

"You whore! You stupid worthless cunt of a mother!"

"You who preferred your younger daughter over your son!"

"You who looked at Ramon with lust and desire, thinking what could have been if the two of you were married now instead of Lando!"

"Yes bitch! I can see right through your soul!"

HAHAHAHA

HAHAHAHAHA

Her guards are down and felt defenseless inside. No answer came out of her heart against these wild accusations except a sob and a tear.

"In the Names of our Lord and savior Jesus Christ"

"Devil tell me your name!!!!"

"tell me your name?

tell you my name?

brahahaha!!!"

NAME! NAME! NAME! NAME!

HAHAHAH!!!!

I admired the patience and perseverance I see in Fr. Reyes' eyes. No trace of desperation nor frustration surfaced in his eyes, which is a sign of a strong faith.

"Get me a spoon", commanded Fr. Reyes.

We were running short of holy water so he decided to use everything with one final blow. He plunge the spoon in to his mouth to get it to open and poured the entire remaining holy water causing his mouth to boil.

"What is your name demon?!!!"

"ABADDON!!!!!!!!!!!!!!!!!!!!!"

The last hurrah proved out to be effective, for the devil finally reveals its identity.

Next, he makes the sign of the cross over himself and the on James, places the end of the stole on his neck, and, putting his right hand on the his head, he says the following in accents filled with confidence and faith:

"Abddon! I cast you out, unclean spirit, along with every Satanic power of the enemy, every spectre from hell, and all your fell companions; in the name of our Lord Jesus +Christ.

Begone and stay far from this creature of God.+ For it is He who commands you, He who flung you headlong from the heights of heaven into the depths of hell. It is He who commands you, He who once stilled the sea and the wind and the storm.

Hearken, therefore, and tremble in fear, Satan, you enemy of the faith, you foe of the human race, you begetter of death, you robber of life, you corrupter of justice, you root of all evil and vice; seducer of men, betrayer of the nations, instigator of envy, font of avarice, fomentor of discord, author of pain and sorrow."

"IN THE HOLY NAME OF JESUS CHRIST, SON OF THE FATHER, BEGONE!!!"

Swarm of flies escaped from the mouth of James, it was disgusting, there were just too many of them. He levitated until the last fly escaped from his mouth, then he suddenly dropped to the floor and became unconscious.

I tried to follow the insects but they escaped through the vents, and soon everything was out of sight.

The next morning I grabbed my newspaper and sipped my morning coffee. The front page reads,

"Japanese Tourist Attacked by a Swarm of Fly inside a popular mall"

It was a good thing that Fr. Reyes s close with the mall owner and agreed to keep the incident low to protect James and the malls reputation. When James woke up, he told us what he felt during the time of the exorcism. He said he could not remember anything except that he trapped inside a cave, tied to a wall, where a devil would enter from time-to-time to torment him.

Hitting him with a long whip made out of barbwire, taking a bite from his skin, or setting his feet on fire. All those times he only longed to be with his family again, he prayed to God to give him one last chance, and he would change his ways.

James is now one of the leaders of the congregation. He is now a powerful speaker preaching the word of God, a living proof of God's mercy and salvation.

CHAPTER XIII

THE HAUNTED DOLL

*T*his part of the book is a real story that happened somewhere in the Northern part of Cebu.

To protect the identities of the people involved, no real names of people, establishments, and places have been mentioned.

Stories of haunted dolls go way back ancient Egypt when enemies of Ramesses III tried to use wax images of his likeness to bring about his death. There are two types of haunted dolls, they can either be haunted dolls, or dolls used in voodoo. Voodoo dolls are used in rituals to curse and inflict pain to anyone who bore their resemblance.

The story I'm about to impart is about a haunted doll. Several haunted dolls have been reported worldwide throughout the ages and several others have not, some experiences are just too traumatic for families that they choose to bury the story in a cave of forgetfulness rather than sharing their stories and reliving the horror. We have Robert the doll, Anabelle, Letta the doll, Okiku, Pupa, and several others which are unreported.

This is one of those you've never heard of, this is a story of a pastor, a haunted doll, and a family. Ciara is a twenty-six year old entertainer in Japan who came from a very poor family in Cebu Philippines. A father with tuberculosis, a mother who washes clothes for a living, and a jobless brother with two children forced her to migrate to Japan and work as an entertainer in a club.

At first it was hard for her to accept that she was now a creature of the night, a prey towards men who are enslaved by their lust for female flesh. She had to endure all this for the betterment of life, for an amount she will never earn if she'd never left Philippines and work a normal job parallel to her educational attainment. Her three years of dancing, and sleeping with different men haven't gone in to waste, for fruits of her unsavory labor has its fruits.

Back in Cebu she already has a three story concrete house, her family was now able to eat three times a day, she was able to send her nephew to a private school, and send balik-bayan box to them every Christmas. A balikbayan box (literally "repatriate box") is a corrugated box containing items sent by overseas Filipinos (known as "balikbayans"). Though often shipped by freight forwarders specializing in balikbayan boxes by sea, such boxes can be brought by Filipinos returning to the Philippines by air. She spends an entire year, saving, collecting, and storing goods so she can send it to her family every December.

In Japan, pre-loved items are disposed by displaying them out your front door for others who wanted them to collect. Most of the times, Filipnos living in Japan are the ones who are able to take advantage of this opportunity. That is why every time Ciara goes to work, she loves walking towards this neighborhood and looking at stuff she can take home, so anything that may be of value will be added to her balikbayan box.

One stormy night, she woke up to the irritating sound of her alarm beeping. She rose from her bed trying to collect her wits, she was alone in a deep blanket of darkness. There was something particularly eerie about that night, it could be the sound of the thunder which sounded like a roar from an angry sky, or the clouds covering the moon which made the night lonely like all hopes were gone, or the heavy drops of rain grudgingly hitting the roof, whatever it was, she doesn't know, she couldn't explain it. There was just a dark heavy feeling lurking inside her heart. It's as if something was telling her not to go work and go back to bed, or say every prayer she ever memorized. Being a Filipino, she was hard working and couldn't bear to lose the amount of money she could be earning that night so she rose from her bed, stormed in to the shower room and dismiss this feeling as a lack of caffeine in her blood.

After shower, she grabbed a cup of coffee from the kitchen and decided to sit a while facing the window. The darkness outside allowed her reflections to be visible which she has been unconsciously staring at. After her first sip of the hot treat her senses came back and she soon realized that it wasn't her face reflecting in the window. At first, she thought someone must be staring at her from outside the window, but that thought was dismissed when the reflection moved as she did. No wonder it was hers, but that face s just so different. It had a long straight black hair which covers almost half of the face, deep black lonely eyes escaping through the strands of the hair, and thin pail lips which are most definitely not hers. She rubbed her eyes to clear her visions and took a second look. She was now looking at her real face.

"Boy am I still sleepy?"

She got dressed and was staring at her make up kit, contemplating whether she should just get to work first before painting herself. She decided not to put on her make up as she was afraid of t being washed away by the heavy rain, plus, she was also afraid of looking at the mirror, fearing that she might see another face again. She opened her door and noticed that the rain has now subsided. Just as she turned around and locked the door, the phone rang..

Krrringgggg.

Kringgg.

"That's strange, who could be calling at this time of the night?"

She grabbed her keys from her pocket and opened the door. Just as she swung the door open, the phone stopped ringing. She waited awhile for the phone to ring again, but it never did. Few drops of rain began to fall again from the dark sky so she took out and opened her umbrella and headed out the empty street. It was still around seven in the evening, but due to the sour weather, most people decided to hide in the coziness of their homes. This made her a bit hesitant to go to work, the bar might be empty and no costumers to entertain, the horrible look of her boss's face flashed in to her mind, giving her a monologue of curses for being absent from work. This was enough motivation to get her going.

It was a fifteen minute walk from her house to the train station so she figured she might get there before the heavy rain lashes again, but she was wrong. The moment she stepped in to the street the rain suddenly poured from the sky with all its might. It was as if a dam broke from the heavens allowing a massive amount of water to fall from the skies. She tightened her grasp towards her umbrella, while her other hand was tacked inside the pocket of her long leather jacket as continue to walk towards her usual route. She loves passing by this neighborhood as mentioned earlier, but things were different tonight, that favorite route was flooded. Might have been as deep as her knee so she was forced to take a detour to an unusual route.

As much as she can, she tried to avoid this neighborhood due to rumors of horror stories going around the neighborhood, but tonight she had no choice. The night was getting colder and her steps were particularly heavy. All of the houses she passed by have their lights off, even the street lights were off except for the one near the end of the road. As she passed by the second house, she noticed water splashing from behind her. She looked back as she walked and noticed what looked like a silhouette of a person standing in the middle of the road, creepily looking up in the sky as if it was drinking from the heavy rain pouring. This gave her a very strange sensation, the hair from the back of her neck started rising, goosebumps everywhere.

This time, she took long hasten steps, and realized that sound of water splashing was going on again. She looked back as she continue walking, she was almost running now. Her bones almost jumped out of her skin when she realized that the silhouette was now walking towards her. Lightning caused a momentary shed of light, and what she saw even made her skin crawl even more. It was a man with a deep sad eyes, tilting his head side-to-side with a mysterious insidious smile painted in his lips, exposing crooked broken teeth. She continued running, and every time she looks back the man was getting closer and closer. What she heard next caused her to momentarily lose her wits, as a strange cackle whispered through the back of her ears causing her feet to tangle, and her to fall to the ground. She finally came in to her senses and realized that the rain suddenly stopped, she looked left to right and saw no sign of that man following her. The surrounding was not so dark anymore as she realized how she finally reached the end of the road with the only street lamp. A smile escaped her lips, thinking she must have imagined all of it when suddenly something caught her attention.

In front of the house with the only working street light, lies a glowing beauty just sitting there in-front of the lawn. It was a beautiful one-foot porcelain geisha doll. It was placed inside a glass box just sitting there waiting for her to pick-up. Not wasting any time, she immediately picked it up and examined the details. Boy, it was in mint condition. Dress looked like it was sewn just yesterday, hair was silky black that glows from the light, face as white as snow, and her red-blood lips made her feel like she was the luckiest girl for finding it.

The doll was heavy so she decided to head back home and leave it there before going to work. She most certainly cannot afford any extra weight on her journey home from her work, she'd be tired as hell by then.

She went inside of her house and turned the light on, boy it became more beautiful with the details coming in to life.It seems strange that with all the heavy rain pouring this doll never got wet, not even the glass. Oh well, she placed it on the shelf and looked at her watch, she was almost late. She turned off the light, locked the doors, and went on her way. Her heart was beating fast thinking of the curses that will be coming out of her boss's mouth for being late. Just as she stepped in to the street, out of her gate, the lights in her house was blinking on and off. Her eyebrows met but she decided to continue running.

When she got home from work, she just slammed the door, threw her bag in the floor, and crashed on the sofa. She was so tired that she could feel her entire body pumping with every beat of her heart. Her hand dropped to her side and it landed on something hard. She turned her head to see what it was, and to her surprise, it was the doll sitting in the sofa, out of the glass. What was it doing there? Who moved it? Maybe it was her housemate, maybe she saw the doll and was admiring its beauty and forgot to return it back to the box. That was the last thing in her mind before finally falling asleep...

Half-way through November and her balik-bayan box is now ready and full. Shoes for her brother and father, make up kit for her mother and sister in-law, lotion, chocolates, candies, and toys for her niece and nephew. One other thing, she was sending the doll to the Philippines. She wrapped it in a bubble wrap, and securely placed it inside a box where it will be safe. She did not include the glass for it might break.

"Mom, when the package gets there, I want papa to make a shelf in the corner of the living room, also, buy a glass box which can fit my one-foot doll I'm sending. It would look good there in the living room."

"ok Ciara, I'll do that. Thank you for all these gifts baby"

"You're welcome mom".

Ciara's housemate, Gym-gym arrived and noticed the doll was no longer in its usual spot.

"Ciara, I'm glad you finally decided to get rid of that doll, it was creeping me out"

"Why Gym? I think it was very beautiful"

"I don't know, maybe I'm just imagining things"

"What? Tell me?"

"Okay, but don't think I'm crazy ok?"

"There was one time when I was taking a shower and while I was washing my hair, the lights suddenly started flickering. It was turning on and off. I thought it was just the bulb so I wanted to switch it off and just use my cellphone. I washed my hair and grabbed the towel, then stepped out of the tub. Suddenly the light turned back on and stopped flickering. I froze to where I was standing when I saw what was sitting there in the covered toilet seat, it was that doll. It looked like its dull lifeless eyes were staring at me directly. It wasn't there when I first entered the bathroom. I got so scared that I ran out immediately"

"That wasn't the only thing that happened. One time I was getting ready for work, putting on my make up in front of the mirror when I noticed a small hand waving at me in my back. I quickly turned around to see what it

was. Then there it was again, sitting in my bed. That horrid doll was looking at me, but this time it put on an evil smile. Something that haunts me every night. Since then I've been sleeping in my friend's house and only come here to pick up some stuff. I'm really glad you got rid of it"

Ciara's serious look suddenly changed and she laughed hysterically.

"hahahahah hahahahah, you don't expect me to believe such non-sense right? And I didn't get rid of it, I sent it to my house in the Philippines so they can put it on display it in my living room"

"Well, I don't care if you don't believe me, but you better ask your parents to watch out for that doll"

"hehehe, whatever. Anyway, have you eaten? I've cooked something"

After almost a month, the box finally arrived in the Philippines. Her parents, brothers, in-laws, and the kids got their shares. The glass where the doll was to be placed was also ready. Pasita, the mother of Ciara went to church last Sunday and handed the pastor some chocolates and canned good from Ciara's box. The pastor was all smiles but upon receiving the goods, he had a sudden vision of a devil causing him to accidentally drop the goods to the floor. The pastor felt a malevolent presence that came back to the Philippines along with the rest of the stuffs. It wasn't long for Pasita and the rest of the family to experience paranormal things around the doll.

One night, Guardo, the father of Ciara went down the kitchen for a glass of water. Sleepily tip-toeing down the stairs to avoid waking everyone, he was yawning when suddenly something caught his attention. There was a pair of red glowing lights inside the glass where the doll was placed. He didn't realize that the doll had lights so he slowly walked towards it, studying it with every step he took. When he was close enough, he realized that it was he doll's eyes that were glowing. The pretty innocent smile was now giving him a sinister look with its glowing red eyes. Its evil smile exposing its demonic looking teeth, with sharp fangs that looked like it can tear any kind of skin it bites. Guardo rubbed his eyes to make sure he was not dreaming and slowly walked a little closer to see clearer. He was now inches away, and this time he was sure it was real. The doll suddenly jumped, ready to attack him but it was blocked by the glass. Guardo fell and quickly ran upstairs and hid himself in under the blanket. His heart was pacing fast, sweat dripping down his forehead, and he was breathing heavily. Pasita never noticed anything. Guardo felt a heavy object on top of his stomach causing him to barely breathe.

"Pacita, get your feet off of my stomach, I can't breathe"

"What are you talking about, I'm facing away from you"

Guardo realized it wasn't his wife's foot so he gently slid the covers from his face. The room was dark but the faint light coming from the windows was enough for him to see clearly. His face is now exposed and he slowly looked at what was sitting in his stomach. And there it was, the haunted doll, looking at him with an evil face. It let out an evil cackle. It raised its hand, and Guardo realized it was holding something. He never found out what it was as the sudden swing to his head knocked him out unconscious. The next morning, he woke up with a throbbing pain in the head. His wife was already up and already going about her daily routine. Still feeling a little banged up, he suddenly remembered what transpired the night before and quickly ran downstairs only to see that the doll was sitting in its usual spot. Did he imagine everything that happened? He tried to dismiss everything but was watchful of the doll since then.

Pasita was cleaning the living room when she noticed the doll was not inside the glass so she called on her granddaughter.

"Elsie. Did you play with the doll?"

"No lola {lola- grandma in Filipino language}"

"Then why is it not here?"

"I don't know lola. Maybe it came out to play. She always ask me to play with her"

"Who?"

"The doll lola. She said she was my friend and she wants to play with me. I have to go lola, I want to play with the other kids"

"Be careful ok? And come back when I call you"

Pasita didn't mind what her granddaughter was saying, thinking it was just child's play. She went to the comfort room to relief herself but when she went back to the living room to continue cleaning, the TV was already along with the electric fan. His grandson was at school, his son and daughter-in-law are in the market, and his husband is out with his friends. She could also see through the window that her granddaughter was busy playing with the other kids. She know she was alone, she slowly walked towards the living room. What she saw left her in puzzle and confusion, for she could not understand what she just saw.

The doll was now sitting in the sofa with the remote beside it and the electric fan facing its direction. Its head was also facing towards the TV as if it was watching the TV show. She asked her granddaughter whether it was her who came in to the house and placed the doll there. With all honesty and innocence reflecting on her eyes, the child calmly denied what her grandmother was questioning. She believed her. Guardo, heard her wife's story and was now sure it was not just his imagination so he also informed her of his experience with the doll. Lately they noticed her granddaughter was always talking to herself. Her grandson doesn't want to stay in the living room alone anymore, he used to watch a lot of TV every time he's at home.

Kringggggg…………
KRrrrrrrrrriinggggggg……..
"kon'nichiwa"
"Hi Ciara, this is your mom"
"Hi mom, how are you?"
"We're good. How are you Ciara? Are you eating enough?"
"I'm good mom, I've just been busy lately. How is everyone? Did you all enjoy the contents of the balik-bayan box?"
"haha, yes Ciara we all loved what you sent. Although I couldn't understand some of the contents. The soap you sent would not produce bubbles, what was its name.. "Mochi' yes the Mochi. I don't know about that soap, it just wouldn't bubble. Then there was that moisturizing milk, it tasted sour and it was so thick. I think it was rotten, it gave me a bad tummy for days."
"Oh mom, the mochi was a food and the moisturizing milk was a lotion"
"Ohhhh, was it? Hahaha"
"Anyway, Ciara, I have a question about that doll"
---beeeeeeepppppp----
The line suddenly went dead.
Ciara called her back.
"Hi mom, sorry the line suddenly went dead"
"that's alright, yes, as I was saying. That doll"
-beepppppeeeeeeeeeeeppppp---------

The line went dead again. She tried calling her mother back but there was no dial tone. Pasita also tried calling her but could not get through too so she sent her a text message instead. *"Ciara, there's been a lot of things going on since the doll arrived. Where did you get it from?"* Upon reading the text message her mom sent, Ciara was taken aback and remembered what Gym-gym told her. She replied to her mom and inquired more about the doll. Pasita told her everything that have happened. Her cellphone suddenly died, that's weird since she just re-charged the battery. She tried to turn it back on, suddenly the video of the doll cackling popped out from the screen and the phone died again. She was so surprised that she accidentally threw her cellphone.

All of a sudden, the lights went dead. A cold wind blew through the back of her neck. Her skin was starting to get goosebumps and a cold feeling ran down her spine. The darkness was so eerie that she could not see anything. A soft laughter broke the silence. She listened to make sure it wasn't coming from the outside. The laughter was starting to get louder and louder by the second until and evil laugh filled the entirety of the room. She curled in the corner of her bedroom, the laughter seemed to be echoing from all directions. Things were being thrown from one side to another and Ciara was just there in the corner, crying. She was so scared she did not know what to do.

A warm hand suddenly held her arms and dragged him outside the room, she was violently trying to shake away the hand when she realized who it was. It was Gym-gym. They made it out of the house alive and she just hugged her. She was crying.*"You were right Gym-gym, you were right"*

Police came to investigate, they got a call from a neighbor due to noise complain. They made a search on the entire house but nothing was found. No force entry. No trespasser, no nothing. She tried to explain to them with all honesty which made them suspect she was on drugs. They were all laughing at her story except for one officer. The police decided to go back to the station and he requested to stay behind. He was watching them and waited for the police car to disappear in to the darkness of the night. They are now out of sight, he can now carry out his concern. With a serious face, he looked in to her eyes, and in his broken English he asked,

"Where do you say you found doll?"

"Why? do you know anything about it?"

"Maybe"

"I picked it up in one of the houses down that neighborhood. Why?"

"It's finally back to where it came from"

"What do you mean?"

The officer took off his jacket and wrapped it around Ciara's arms. He invited them to go inside so he can share the story.

There was a newlywed couple who came to the Philippines for their honeymoon. During their vacation something happened with the wife, she was attacked by a swarm of flies while they were strolling in the mall. It was even reported all over the news. A swarm of flies went inside her mouth.

"All of it?"

"Yes, all flies, go to inside her mouth, in her nose, in her ears, everywhere"

"That's disgusting"

"Yes, when they go to doctor, they checked but could not find any trace. They come back here in Japan and since then, the wife acting very strange. We always getting call from their house due to fighting couple. The last call we responded, the wife killed husband and then she suicide. When we arrived, their house full of blood and the doll was inside the glass box sitting there right below where the wife was hanging. I looked at the doll and I swear it winked at me"

The police described how the doll looked like and Ciara almost fainted. The doll she sent to her family was exactly the same doll they found. Her heart was filled with sadness and remorse, it's as if she sent an insidious terror upon her family. Tears filled her eyes, sobbing, she borrowed Gym-Gym's phone and sent a text message to her mother.

"Ma, burn it"

Pacita was out talking to her neighbor. Her husband was out with his friends, his grandson in school, while his son and his wife in the market selling goods. It was just her and her granddaughter who was busy playing with the neighborhood kids. They were busy exchanging rumors{chismis}, which is a very favorite past time habit amongst Filipinos. She had a glimpse of their attic and noticed a small hand waving. It made her mad, it could be her granddaughter again middling with Ciara's stuff. They kept the attic off limits since it is Ciara's room and the stairs heading there is very steep for the children. Hasty steps she took as she walked towards their house, motivated to give her a good scolding when she saw that she was just out their laying with the neighbors. She was taken aback, whose hand could it be then? She realized that she kept that room locked. Slowly, she twisted the door knob, slowly walked inside the house. Cold sweat ran down her forehead as she grabbed the keys to the room. Her steps were slow and sure. She did not know what to expect, except to satisfy the thirst of her curiosity. The wooden stairs creaked with every step she took towards the attic. Something was telling her not to go but she did not listen to it. She used the key and slowly pushed opened the door. It let out a squeak. The sound made her even more nervous and made her want to wet her pants. What she saw made her heart drop. The doll was standing by the window on top of a chair waving outside. She was so shocked that she just stood there frozen in fear. Slowly and creepily, the head of the doll turned towards her with an evil smile and red glowing eyes. Pacita tried to turn back when the door suddenly shut close. She ran towards the door and was crying, begging, screaming for help. The doll slowly got down from the chair and was creepily walking towards her.

"Hyehahehehehe"

It let out an evil laugh that sounded like it was coming from a witch. Pacita dropped to the floor and crawled towards the corner of the room. Screaming, crying, and hysterically begging for help. The doll was slowly walking towards her, with a shining thing on its hand. What was it? As the doll came nearer, it became clearer, it was holding a very sharp kitchen knife. Pacita's heart chest was tightening, her breath became heavy, and it was evident that she was having a heart attack. The doll was now right next to her feet. It raised the knife and was about to stab her when the door suddenly swung open. Guardo came back and heard her screaming so he quickly climbed upstairs and kicked the door open. He saw his wife dropped to the floor holding with her hand squeezing her chest, desperately trying to catch her breath. The doll rolled inside the bed leaving the knife behind. He took her downstairs, sat her in the couch, and gave her a breathing space for her to catch her breath. By the grace of the Lord she was alright.

"Did you catch it?"

"Caught what?"

She was still catching her breath while pointing towards the glass box where the doll used to be located. When Guardo looked towards its direction, he was no longer surprised to see that it was empty. He grabbed her cellphone so he can tell his son to come home and help him find the doll.

That's when he found out that an unfamiliar number texted her wife saying, "Ma, burn it" He understood who it was from. Moments later his son arrived and they went upstairs to look for the doll. Armed with a baseball bat, laundry paddle, and fear in their hearts, they slowly climb the empty wooden stairs. They reached the door and slowly pushed the door open. There was silence. No movement from the room. Guardo remembered how it suddenly ran under the bed so he pointed towards its direction. He gave a signal for his son to be ready as he was going to flip the bed up. His son tightened his grip on the bat. Sweats racing from his forehead.

"crasshhahssshhh"

He flipped the bed and the doll was just lying there, motionless, and lifeless. They bought it outside so they can burn it. Guardo threw it in the middle of an empty lot and sprinkled kerosene all over it. He took out his lighter and prepared to burn it. A strong wind blew and his lighter wouldn't lit. Desperately trying to crank it again and again but it just won't work. His son, picked up his bat again and was ready to swing to break it when his daughter Elsie suddenly hugged the doll to protect it.

They grabbed her to take her away from the doll but when they turned her around. Her eyes were deep and dark, her skin was pale, and her lips became black and broken. She screamed at them and ran towards the house. Neighbors who witnessed the events became scared that they decided to call on the pastor. The entire family of Guardo emptied the house, they all just stood there outside, waiting for the pastor. They remembered the doll, Guardo picked it up and looked at its eyes. Now it was nothing more than a lifeless porcelain object with cold eyes, and painted smile. It was evident that the evil lurking inside it was now transferred to the little girl. The pastor came and everyone just started talking and pointed at the house. He got confused with all of them talking, screaming, and fuzzing that he immediately went in to the house and opened the door. He was met by the little girl Elsie.

"Hi pastor"

He looked towards the direction of the crowd and everyone was pointing at the little girl with concern on their faces.

"What's going on Elsie?"

"I don't know about them pastor, they want to hurt me"

"Okay, just stay their inside while sort this out"

The pastor closed the door behind him and went to the crowd.

"Okay I need you all to be quiet so I can talk to the family. Now what happened here?"

Pacita emerged from the crowd and walked towards the pastor. She explained things to him and while she was explaining, he remembered that day she handed her chocolates and goods from Japan.

Now that he understood what was going on, he became a little nervous. It was his first time to encounter real evil. Armed with prayers and determination to help the little girl, he slowly paced back in to the house. He grabbed the door knob and unlocked the door. Slowly pushing the door open, he vigilantly stepped inside. No little girl to meet him this time. He found her curled in the kitchen corner, rocking in the floor back and forth.

"Satan you deceiver, let go of that little girl"

The possessed girl slowly moved its head to face him, her body still curled up in the floor. He looked in to her red insidious glowing eyes, her stair was piercing right to his soul. His body became cold and fear overtook his heart. His knees became weak that he could barely stand. At that moment, he became so ashamed towards the Lord, for he feared like he never had faith at all. The girl was screaming at him in a deep growling voice, in a language he does not understood. He tried to open his mouth but his lips and tongue were dry and his throat cracked. The evil he was facing smelled his fear and laughed at him. The laugh was so horrible and scary. He regained his composure.

"Help me oh Lord, make me an instrument towards this little girl's salvation"

"In the Name of The Lord Jesus Christ, devil I command you to release this little girl"

I am not afraid of you for I am with the Lord,

Mark 16:17-18 says "And these signs shall follow them that believe; In my name shall they cast out devils; they shall speak with new tongues; They shall take up serpents; and if they drink any deadly thing, it shall not hurt them; they shall lay hands on the sick, and they shall recover." kjv

"wraaAAaaaaahhh"

She stood from the floor and levitated towards him, about to attack. He was protected by an invisible force that she could not get past to. Wind blew and the windows swung open. A swarm of fly flew from her mouth and was attacking the pastor. Guardo and his son ran to help him while Pacita sobbed while watching the events unfold.

They were able to shoo the flies away and helped the pastor get back on his feet.

"In the Name of The Lord Jesus Christ, tell me your name demon"

Bwaahahaha name name name game

Hahaha

"you are subject to the Name of the Lord, tell me your name"

"Abaddonnnn"

"Pacita, bathe that goat with kerosene"

"Yes pastor"

In the Philippines, raising a goat is common and each family usually have one tied to the backyard.

"Just as the apostle Paul did in Acts 16:16-18, "I command you in the name of Jesus Christ to come out of her."

Elsie's body was wildly shaking and it was levitating from the ground. The power of the devil was not match with the faith and determination burning from the heart of the pastor.

"I command you devil, release the girl and transfer to the body of that goat"

The wind suddenly stopped blowing and Elsie fell down to the floor. Swarm of flies escaped from her mouth and went inside the goat's ears, mouth, and nose. Her father held Elsie in his arms. She was so wet with sweats, but her face now look normal.

Meanwhile, the goat violently shook and broke the tie and began charging towards the pastor. Guardo quickly jumped towards the goat trying to stop it but it met him with its horn and was thrown several feet away. Some of the brave neighbors, tried to hold on to the leash of the goat. Guardo broke a rib and it pierced his left lung, Pacita came to his aid. She cried when she realized how badly he was bleeding. He weakly grabbed his cigarette from his pocket, took out his Zippo and lit his cigar.

The goat drawn its attention again towards the pastor, with smoke coming out of its nose, raging eyes glowing in red. He was like a bull getting ready to attack the matador. With his dying breath, Guardo threw the lit zippo lighter towards the goat and it burst in to flame.

An evil scream that sounded like it was coming from hell itself filled the entire community. Flame glazed several feet in to the air taking shape in to, what looked like a devil's face. The flame died when the bull turned into ashes.

Ciara arrived a few days later only to attend her father's funeral. They sold every property they had in that place and moved to a new town, trying to move on and start a new life away from the horror they've experienced.

In a nearby area, a resort was being constructed. White sand beach and green palm trees, this is perfect for tourist.

One of the workers was digging a hole when he hit something like a glass buried in the ground. He put down his shovel and dug it using his hand. After several minutes, it finally came to sight. A beautiful porcelain Japanese doll placed inside a glass box. "This will be a perfect gift for my daughter", says he o himself.

CHAPTER XIV

EMBRACING THE CURSE IV

Mathilda!!!!!

This is the last name that every motorist hear before every accident. This old woman whispers this last word before each accident occurs. Some victims are lucky to have survived while some do not. In the crowded streets of the downtown area, there's one place motorist dare not pass during midnight. Rumor says that this area is haunted; a ghost of a woman who hitches rides or suddenly crosses the street is causing numerous accidents. Back in the late 80s, there was an elderly woman who was limping as she crossed the street when a speeding drunk driver hit her, throwing her into the side walk.

It was a horrible fall and the woman couldn't possibly survive with her skull cut open and her brain scattered all over the street. Since then, these terrible apparitions and accidents started happening.

Motorist reported an old woman wearing a veil covered in blood would try and hitch a ride. Motorist are too afraid to stop but when they looked behind them, the woman was already riding with them. The woman would then blurt out the word Mathilda before drivers black out. Some reported a white figure would suddenly cross the street causing accidents when they try to avoid it.

One rainy night, Roger was not in the mood to drive his cab. His blood pressure was high but with the constant nagging of his wife who reminded him of the upcoming bills and class opening was becoming suffocating.

He stood up and grabbed his jacket then headed for the door. Drowsing as he stepped in to his cab and turned on the engine. He didn't want to turn on the vehicle's air conditioner but this most of the passengers would complain about it so he had no choice. The temperature is causing the windshield to be blurry and the heavy drops of the rain makes it a zero visibility trip. Roger's eyes are dropping. He tried his best to keep himself awake and to focus with his driving but to no avail. He doze off..

"THUG!!!"

He woke up to the sound or a motion of something hit by his vehicle. He was so nervous and shivering as he exited his vehicle. With that strong of a hit it would surely kill any living being unfortunate enough to be on the receiving end. What a relief when he found out that there was nothing there. He looked everywhere, through the muddy and flooded street but there was no sign of anything. He decided to jump back in his vehicle. He felt a sigh of relief as he inhaled a deep air trying to catch his breath and normalize his palpitating heart. He was about to start the engine when he noticed something in the rear-view mirror. It was as if a black pile of garbage is seated in the backseat. He quickly turned around to see what it was. To his horror a blooded woman wearing a veil whose face has been tragically misplaced and broken was sitting there trying to hand him a piece of paper. The woman was sobbing and his voice was shivering as it keeps repeating the name Mathilda!!! Mathilda!!!! Mathilda!!!!!

Roger felt a pressure spreading from his chest to his arms, to his neck, and to his jaw. He couldn't breathe now as his chest where tightening.

Cring!!!

Cring!!!

Cring!!!

I woke up to sound of my cellphone. I answered and it was Christian. He was asking me if I can accompany him to the morgue to see his brother who died of a heart attack while driving his cab. I didn't say no, I knew how much he is in need of a company. We arrived in Saint Joseph Aguilar Funeral homes around 3pm and the receptionist showed us the way to the morgue.

Christian couldn't hold his tears as he saw his brother's body lying their lifeless and cold. I put my arms around his shoulder to let him know that everything's gonna be alright. He was now crying hysterically and I accidentally touched his brother's foot while trying to calm him down.

Out of nowhere someone or something blurted out the name "Mathilda!" I looked around the room but here was no one else there. It was just me, Christian, and Roger's lifeless body. I noticed that Roger was holding a piece of paper.

I went a little closer. It looked like it was a very old piece of paper given that it's already yellowish and it looked like it was still encoded from a "type writer".

The moment I touched the paper I dropped to the floor and saw a vision of an old woman limping. She was in a hurry and was trying to cross the street when a vehicle hit her and she died. Another vision came to me and saw that the same woman who was now blood bathe was in the back seat of Roger's cab and handed him this note before he had a heart attack.

Upon regaining my consciousness, I checked the paper. It looked like an old school examination permit for the University of Ubec, the same school where I attended high school. It was for a Mathilda Navarro. I noticed that the year reads 1987?

Why would this woman hand Roger a 1987 examination permit for a Mathilda Navarro? My head was filled with questions so I slipped the note in my pocket and went back to comforting my friend. One of the theories I have in mind is that Roger must have impregnated a woman from his past life, but that would be impossible since he would have been a teenager by then. Another theory I had was that, it might have been Roger driving the vehicle who hit the woman instantly killing her. Maybe I was just overthinking and this spirit was simply asking for his help. I know Christian has a lot in his plate right now so I didn't tell him anything yet.

I went to the area where his cab was found parked and where they found him lifeless. I didn't see anything out of the ordinary. I was so eager to get the answer I was looking for so I waited till dark. It was around 9 Pm, this was perfect for me. I took out a candle, lit it, and took out the note from my pocket. I closed my eyes and said,

"I am here. I'm just here to talk"

When I opened my eyes, there was darkness all around me. It was so dark that it felt like I fell in to a dark and very deep pit. The candle was not enough to bring brightness to my surrounding. The silence was deafening that I could even hear the sound of my breath and my heart beating. From my right a figure was slowly creeping out of the darkness. It looked like a woman with a disfigured body. She was cover in blood and mud as she slowly crawl towards me. Each movement she did created the sound of broken bones cracking. Her movement was so slow and dragging that it creeps me out more and more.

More bone cracking sound this time as her figure tried to stand up on front of me revealing her true figure. Her broken skull and popping eyes were coming together and the blood dripping in all over her body are coming back inside her body. It was like watching a horrible disfiguration being played back, I felt like I was about to throw up.

"POP"

I couldn't help it. After I threw up and wiped my face. The woman was now standing in front of me without the wounds and blood splattered face. Her face looked so calm and kind. You wouldn't believe the entity standing in front of you was the cause of so many vehicular accidents, claiming the life of dozen men. I asked her what was wrong and who was Mathilda Navarro. She just kept staring at me, mouth shut with a blank expression on her face.

Then her hands started reaching for my head. There was no sign of aggression so I didn't dodge. When her hands reached my head, I was quickly swallowed in to great bright light.

I was in an old small house. From the looks of the place, I know I was in the slums. The lady was busily preparing breakfast while her daughter was blankly staring out the window. She was so lost in her deep thoughts that by the looks on her face you would know that something was bothering her. Her mother had to shake her out of her thoughts.

"Mathilda!"

"What's wrong honey? Are you okay?"

Mathilda suddenly cried and gave her mother a big hug.

"What's wrong baby?"

"Nothing mom, I'm just nervous with this exam"

"I have your examination permit here, I'll just lay it on the table while you eat your breakfast"

She looked at the table and there was only 1 hotdog, a glass of milk, and a cup of rice.

"Mom, let's eat?"

Her mother's tummy growled but she had to lie for there wasn't enough food for the both of them.

"I already ate honey, you go ahead and eat"

Her mother said goodbye to her daughter and went out to do laundry for their neighbors.

After washing the neighbor's clothes she went inside and noticed that Mathilda's food was untouched and the examination permit was sitting there in the table. This was the same slip I found in roger's hand. She hastily grabbed the piece of paper, slipped it in her pocket and ran towards the door hoping to catch up with Mathilda.

She accidentally stepped on a sharp object and her foot started bleeding. She continued walking. She didn't care if her leg was hurting, she need to give the slip to her daughter, and otherwise, she might not be able to take her exams. Back then, there might have been lesser number of vehicles since she was confident in crossing the streets without even looking. Limping and skipping, traveling in a haste. She was in a much hurry that she didn't notice a speeding vehicle heading towards her direction. Late was it when she heard the vehicle's beep and she was already thrown in to the curb. There lays the woman. Bleeding. Lifeless. Holding the slip in her hand. The driver sped and left the scene.

I was drawn back to reality with the candle on my hand. She was still standing in front of me, she reached for my hand where the slip was located and she said.

"Mathilda!"

I realized that she was trapped in that moment and she did not realize how long it has been since 1987. She want me to give Mathilda the slip. I know what I had to do, I have to find this Mathilda Cortez and give this slip to her. The next day, I went to the university to try and dig some information. Too many scary memories linger in this place. But that was all in the past and that was not why I came here for. I am here with a mission. I know that they are not allowed to divulge these information but I was just pressing my luck. I went to the registrar's office and spoke with a working student. As expected, she wouldn't give me any information. Her superior overheard the name "Mathilda Cortez" and asked me to go to her office. She asked me to sit by her office as she wiped the sweat off her forehead.

"Do you know Mathilda?"

She removed her glasses and wiped the tears from her eyes as she softly spoke.

Yes, I know her. I was her only friend.

That day she killed herself, she left her hanky in her desk and I kept it ever since to remember her.

"Wait, what? Killed herself?" I interrupted

"Yes, she jumped from the sixth floor during our examination day"

She handed me the hanky and the moment it touched my hand, a vision came to me. I knew there was something familiar about Mathilda.

Mathilda stood from the table, still lost in her thoughts, grabbed her bag and walked out the door. She forgot to bring her examination permit. She was not herself. Lost in her deep thoughts, her mind flying in the clouds. However, she did not look like she was daydreaming. She was clearly troubled and problematic, for in every step she took a tear fell from her eyes.

What was bothering her?

She was sitting silently in her desk, suddenly the instructor came in. He was a tall dark man in his mid-40s. He spoke in a deep and audible voice.

"Ready your slips and I'll hand you your questionnaires. Clear your desks and get rid of other stuffs"

"Mathilda Navarro! You are about to fail my class and now you are here without your exam permit?"

"Sorry sir, I left it at home"

"You see, that's why you are about to fail my class because you always forget things! You are so absent-minded and day dreaming."

"I'll let you take the exam but I will not record your score unless I see that permit. If your score goes below 95%, I guarantee you will fail my class.

That statement gave Mathilda goosebumps, she knew she was in danger of failing this subject. She wasn't dull, she just wasn't that interested with History. She thought of her mother who tirelessly washed their neighbor's clothes just so she could send her to school. She thought of her alcoholic father, how he would beat her to death if he finds out. After he was sure that no else was watching, the sneaky professor took out a special test paper from his bag and handed it to Mathilda. This contains a different set of questions devised for her to fail.

When Mathilda opened the test questions, her whole world collapsed. Her heart was beating fast, sweats dropping from her forehead like a water leak, and she could barely breathe. None of the lessons she studied were part of the examination. She tried to answer the papers but the worries and anxiety caused her to mental block. Out of nowhere, Mathilda suddenly stood up and raced out of the class room. She ran in the corridors and jumped off the building. I was awaken by the registrar superior's violent shaking on my shoulder. She thought I was having a seizure. It took some time for me to catch my breath and informed her of why I was there. I don't know if she thought I was crazy, I just knew that I needed that hanky; I need to give it to her mother whose spirit still lingers the streets. With a heavy heart, I asked for her if she could give to me her dead friend's remembrance. Her expressions changed again, sadness painted in her face. She said she heard rumors of a spirit lurking the school, she just knew it was Mathilda. If it would help put her spirit to rest then she would gladly give it to me. She shed a tear before giving it to me. I thanked her and assured her that this would help a lot.

I had a plan in mind, it was a long shot but it was worth taking. Here I go again, in this haunted university, doing my best to stay strong for the sake of these lost souls. I stayed hidden in one of the cubicles of the old comfort room. It was getting dark; I think it was already around 11 pm. This should be enough for the school to be empty. I just realized no one ever came in the comfort room ever since I got in. All of a sudden, the toilet next to the cubicle I was occupying flushed. Weird, I didn't hear any footsteps, nor did I hear the door opening. A cold wind suddenly ran down my neck to my spine. Goosebumps everywhere. I felt like peeing when all of a sudden all of the cubicle doors started opening and banging. The lights turning on and off. A shadowy figure of a man started floating from the door to my direction. This was the same spirit we saw back when I was in high school with my friend. I know who this is. This is the dead professor. The one who died in the fire when the building burned. I was too afraid but I screamed anyway,

"I can help you!!!!"

In a blink of an eye, a burned face of a man whose right eye was dangling from the whole and the teeth are exposed was suddenly in front of me face to face.

"You can't help me!!!!!!!!!!!!"

"I can try"

I know I was too afraid but I had to do it. I slowly lifted arm so I could touch the head of this horrible thing.

Upon touching his head, I felt an explosion in front of me. There was too much brightness; I had to close my eyes. I opened my eyes and everything went back to normal. I was crying, sobbing, and I never felt so much remorse in my heart. I felt very sad and guilty that I didn't notice I was holding a class record in my hand. Mathilda was not failing his class; he was just threatening her to get to her pants. She was a mild and gentle flower, a perfect prey for him. He usually threatens students to fail them if they don't sleep with him. Then a tragedy befell him, came a time when he could no longer have an erection. That is when he realized all the evil things he had done to all his former students. One night, drunk and depressed. He decided to burn himself in his classroom. He only seek forgiveness from Mathilda and all others who became his victims. I realized how rumors spread and lies go with it. Mathilda was not pregnant, he wasn't able to touch him; she just couldn't take the pressure of giving her mother the sad news and the fear of her father beating her. He didn't die because she haunted her, he died by means of suicide due to depression.

This was an important discovery but now I have to proceed with my mission. The once scary professor was now sobbing in the floor, I have to leave him that way, I have to resolve things one at a time. The stairs was not as easy to climb as it was before. I had to catch my breath from time to time. Sweat dripping all over my body. After a lifetime of climbing stairs, I finally made it to the 6th floor.

The wind was cold that night. I don't know if it was my sweat combining with the wind or is it the fear I've been trying to bury inside of me. I was scared to death, my knees were shaking, and cold sweat continue to drop from my head. I took out the candle from my pocket and tried to light it. The cold wind blowing was making it difficult. I need this light to guide the spirit I'm trying to summon. She needs to find her way in to me. I found a corner where the wind cannot reach. I bent down, took out the hanky from my pocket and began praying. After praying, I called on Mathilda's spirit.

"Mathilda"

I tried my best for my voice not to shake, trying to sound confident and with authority calling her name through the candle.

"Mathilda, can you hear me?"

The light of the candle suddenly died. There was darkness. There was silence.

Out of nowhere, the candle began to light like a firework. Intense fire began to blow from the candle and began to take the shape of a woman. The fire was so great that I had to let go of the candle. A strong wind from my back knocked me to the ground, followed by a voice of an enraged spirit echoing through the air.

WHAT.........

DO................

YOU......................

WANT??????????????!!!!!!!!!!!!!!!!!!!!

"Mathilda, I man here to help!"

The wind started to grow stronger blowing papers and dust in to the air. It was blowing me away but I stood firm and reached for my pocket. I waived the slip for Mathilda to see, and screamed...

"YOU, I REMEMBER YOU, I ASKED FOR YOUR HELP BEFORE BUT YOU TURNED YOUR BACK ON ME"

"I'm sorry I was very young back then and didn't know what to do"

"AND YOU ONLY COME BACK NOW? NOW YOU WILL JOIN ME IN DEATH"

Realizing I was not floating in thin air and was slowly heading towards edge of the building. No time to waste, I immediately took out the slip from my pocket.

"Mathilda! This is from your mother!"

Upon mentioning the word, the wind suddenly died and calmness of the night took over the atmosphere. What remains in front of me was a sobbing spirit with a broken skull and a blooded head. She was crying while she was down on her knees. I approached the ghost as she keeps sobbing.

"Mathilda, you can be with your mother now. I can help you. You can now both cross to the next world with her."

Her face became to lighten and her face started to became normal, the violence in her aura subsided. She was such a beautiful girl, too bad her life ended this way.

"What happened to my mama?"

She wept even more knowing that her mother is dead. I presented her with the slip.

"Your mama was in such a hurry trying running towards your school to give you this"

"But I failed her, I was failing my class"

"No Mathilda, you are wrong. Here is a copy of the class record showing you had good grades"

She took the slip and the class record and like a bubble that suddenly blew, she vanished in front of me.

I needed to do one last thing. I was so tired, drained, and exhausted but I am not done yet. I still need to get back to her mother. I must put an end to this and finish what I started.

I went back to site where her mother got hit by the car. I lit the candle again and summoned her spirit. She was standing there in the corner and her spirit started floating from a dark corner of the street, slowly floating to where I was standing. I pulled Mathilda's hanky from my pocket and presented it to her. A blinding light suddenly started to appear that lit the dark and empty street. Then came in to view the spirit of Mathilda. The 2 lost souls finally reunite after years of anguish, haunting, hurt, and horror. The once scary and broken spirits became visions of angels on earth. They walked towards the empty street holding each other's hand and slowly faded in to the darkness of the night until they were out of sight.

EPILOGUE

I was so relieved and felt a sense of fulfilment knowing that Mathilda and Martha's spirits finally found peace. A sense of happiness bloomed inside my heart, no one will ever know what I did, no one needs to, and just assured there will be no hauntings anymore in this side of the street. I took a deep breath, put on a smile in my face and turned back. I thought I was going to get home and finally have my rest, but what lies on front of me tells me that's not gonna happen. Dragging steps, floating in the air, crawling in the mud, these lost souls slowly approaching towards me all have the same word to say;

"Help me!!!!"

But who's this leading in front of them?

Oh it was the burned professor.

"YOU SAID YOU WERE GOING TO HELP ME"

He choke my neck, dragging me towards the middle of the street. It all happened so fast, a beam of light flashing from a car's headlight blinded my sight and the next thing I felt was a piercing pain slowly jolting in my side before I went flying several feet, and finally crashing in the wet pavement, then everything went black.

I woke up in the hospital the next morning with a strap in my head. The nurse was adjusting something in my dextrose, she told me that I was hit by a car but the driver immediately left the scene.

"hit and run?"

"And who brought me here?"

"Two weird looking ladies wearing all white brought you here, the other seem to be the mother and the other was her daughter. They disappeared before the police got their statements"

"Mathilda and Martha"

"did you say something?"

"No, nothing, do you have anything to eat?"

That accident must have injured my pineal gland for I have never seen anything paranormal ever again since then.

Years passed by and I finally have my own family. Carried in my left arm was my 8th month old healthy daughter and my beautiful wife holding on to my other arm. We were happily walking on our way to church when a cold wind blew sending chills down my spine. A familiar chill of fear ran towards my bones. It's been so long since the last time I felt this way. I saw a blurry figure of an old man walking on my left side. I realized who it was, it was the burned professor...He gave me the ugliest evil smile I have ever seen in my whole entire life.....

I was already happy living a normal and peaceful life. It wasn't easy growing up,

Living life in fear, living with a third eye...

Not again, please not again..

I noticed that my daughter was staring at the spirit, following its movement, unable to understand what she was looking at..

I looked at her in the eyes and said to myself,

"Oh No! Please no, not you!"

Printed in the United States
By Bookmasters